FIRE-FLY

Anthea Church

MINERVA PRESS
WASHINGTON LONDON MONTREUX

FIRE-FLY
Copyright © Anthea Church 1995

All Rights Reserved

No part of this book may be reproduced in any form,
by photocopying or by any electronic or mechanical means,
including information storage or retrieval systems,
without permission in writing from both the copyright owner
and the publisher of this book.

ISBN 1 85863 332 X

First Published 1995 by
MINERVA PRESS
1 Cromwell Place
London SW7 2JE

2nd Impression 1995

Printed in Great Britain by
Ipswich Book Company Ltd., Ipswich, Suffolk.

FIRE-FLY

ABOUT THE AUTHOR

Anthea Church is head of English at The Urdang Academy of Ballet and Performing Arts in Covent Garden. Other writings include a book for teachers: *Co-operation in the Classroom*, translated into five languages, and writings on meditation: *Inner Beauty* and *Arts of Life* published initially in Portuguese, now translated into three languages.

Cover design by George Edwards

POEMS

by

Shireen Shaikh

◆

FOREWORD

by

Eugene Romain

ACKNOWLEDGEMENT

When I was writing this book, it was said to me: the best creative work cannot be done on your own. I was offended. I have always liked working on my own and have taken a lot of strength from inhabiting an inner world. But in this context it turned out to be true. Fire-Fly, though in subject matter intensely personal, could neither have been developed nor completed had it not been shared.

Carol Rickard shared Fire-Fly with me. She carried out the most skilled and yet most underestimated task of all, which is editing. By refined and sometimes ruthless adjustments, she opened up a clearer route through the intricate pathways these stories weave. She also typed, printed, researched and communicated with publishers. One cannot do adequate justice to that kind of support.

I should also like publicly to acknowledge a quality in her which I consider ultimately to be greater than any creative achievement. And that is a capacity to care over a long period of time, for what is not on a most obvious level your own. If you take any pleasure from this book, it is very largely due to her ability to care in that way and her stamina in attending to the finer details of its composition.

Anthea Church   July 1994

FOREWORD

Fire-Fly is an astounding read. It is one of those extremely rare journeys which once embarked upon you feel you have always been travelling. I can think of few stories which, so vividly and often painfully, show the extreme and perplexing paradoxes of life, but which remain so positively life-affirming. It is a celebration of great intensity.

The author leads us carefully down into the invisible processes behind life's outer appearance. Just as our bodies mostly run themselves so our souls must do likewise, and generally we remain as oblivious to the workings of our spirits as we do to the workings of our physiologies. If the work at hand is grave enough, energy may need to be drawn from elsewhere, but like a computer network sharing processing power, at the front end virtually nothing is effected. This iceberg self, nine-tenths submerged, is tremendously exciting in Church's hands. We become each a multitude of possible people. She portrays us as beings not of actuality but of possibility. Our variations are so many that they could, as it were, be lined up to make an unseen dynasty into the future.

We are driven by the desire to do justice to these hidden inner stories and this desire may turn to want or need, but the pressure lies ultimately not with ourselves but with life. Life has to deliver to us not vice-versa. I am not the fulfiller of my unrealised dreams, I am the recipient of those fulfilments. I live and receive on behalf of my secret self. I am here today because my requests of yesterday command a response. It is this underlying relationship which many of Church's characters unwittingly have with life that gives such a positive atmosphere to her world. Lionel's awful tribulations, Padma's patience, Corina's intuition, none of these have been wasted. Every drop of it is gathered up and stored. It forms the heritage that is carried inside, and it is against this accumulation that life must measure up if it is to do us justice. Church's book is a pledge, a guarantee that life is and will ultimately be revealed to be supremely valuable and worthwhile - because one's spirit is always owed so much.

Almost from the first page we have someone pushing at the boundaries of his world. And we find that in this book one's world extends inwards as well as outwards. The characters are always pulled between inner and outer worlds. But their real tension is generally between the past and the present. Not yesterday, but the subterranean past, the forces inside that rarely surface but are always pushing. Nomi rebels not against his society but against his identity. He starts off amazed at the sheer oddness of existence - in particular its specificity; that now he has precisely this mother and that father and he is tied to a whole set of relations and conditions which will not dance or change as he dances and changes. He senses that being human is somehow too much of a compromise, too limiting. And although we subsequently discover that in Church's world, life is most certainly not self-defeating, the sense that it is a compromise subsists through much of the book.

The central dilemma of her characters is how to be divine and human at the same time. This question is posed with Nomi and is never truly resolved. Most of Church's other central characters accept the boundaries of their worlds, but it is not without sorrow. We are led to sense ourselves as creatures who are forever reaching backwards as if to some lost memory or a different way of being. The tension that this causes is central to us. We are subjects of time and space whose dreams and sensitivities respect neither. We live in the world and like Nomi are regulated by its intrinsically public nature, but secretly and compulsively we listen for a few words from some other unknown language, for music wafting down from another floor. Being human is obviously natural and inevitable but it is still not an easy thing. It is a funnelling of an ocean through one point, a holding back. It is using a tiny amount of oneself to create the measured ticking of a human mind. It is an unavoidable price - an equation - to be a person means you cannot be truly conscious, truly free or paradoxically truly yourself.

Man is a riddle but, as the rest of Fire-Fly attests, what a glorious riddle. Our antecedents may be beyond the limits of language and certainly Church never tries to peek behind the veil at either end of life. She does not play witchdoctor, and this is a crucial point: she has no need of metaphysics. The massive stature of our spiritual heritage is itself phrased in the exquisite beauty of her characters' lives. Life does not preclude the transcendent, it weaves it into the stuff of you and me!

And this, perhaps above all else is the magic that makes this book sublime. Time and again Church effortlessly makes gaping holes in the firmament and floods the world with such beauty that even my domestic concerns become translucent with ancient purpose and immeasurable promise.

Eugene Romain
June 1994

Contents

		Page
1.	Nomi	17
2.	Sirus	28
3.	Corina	38
4.	Pierre	49
5.	Lionel	60
6.	Lisa	69
7.	Lily	81
8.	Padma	92
9.	Steven	104
10.	God	116
11.	Angel	128
12.	Mother	140
13.	Child	150

NOMI

Do not carve your name
in the tree whose branches craft forgetfulness:
his skill is more ancient than carpentry.

He crept, as though whispering to the stones with his feet, until he was within touching distance of his mother's back. She was seated close to the fire, studying the horizon, hoping for a last burst of warmth from the sun. But it had already begun to drop behind the hills, its heat a cool pink cap over the Eagle's Head.

She began to heave up her body, which appeared to have housed several children; in fact only one, Nomi's, whose brown hand was now tugging on her heavy hide smock.

She swung around and looked up at the face; wished it were not so soft, so small, because inside it was an enchanter. And her instinct, deeper than a mother's, knew that Nomi needed some hard, cool treatment.

"Nomi..." The tone and the silence that followed meant 'go into the shelter'.

He did not move, just kept holding her, even harder; harder than the softness of his skin suggested possible. She swivelled right around as though to enclose and lift him to where she wanted him. Her face was close to his cheek, and she held the silence, using only a gesture to instruct him. Her arm pointed heavy and strong, like the branches that Laus would throw onto the embers later in the evening. Nomi understood, but he wanted a fight.

He knew that his face could win her, and that soon the arm pointing to the hut would embrace him and leave him free to stay up late and play.

It was a face she had not intended. Carrying this child in her womb, she had figured in her mind a tall, angular boy. Instead came this moon face; this face made of wet grass and dew, of melted sunlight and sleep. When she hugged him, he merged into her skin. When he lay in the hollow of a tree, he became its missing bark - as though he did not know how to become himself or was too strange to dare to.

She delayed as he had hoped. Not that he did not want to go into the shelter, lie down and sleep. He enjoyed the freedom of closed eyes. But he wanted to go on with his game: bend his mother's strong form and make it obey him; twist it like a branch, green and sinewy inside; to hurt. It gave him pleasure to break her. Though once done, he would run off with a hardness in his chest which was regret.

"Nomi, Nomi!" There, she had succumbed; had used words; had let her arm fall, ready to touch his small back. Yet she did not. For in this little tussle, she felt his defiance, and her sharp mind instructed distance and caution.

Soon afterwards Laus joined them. Head tilting, palm upturned, his body enquired what they were doing. His mute question told of the distance between them. Underneath his solitude and accuracy - logs always cut to size, laid right, lit carefully - he was worried by the oddness of his son. In a society that exalted moderation, Nomi was too turbulent, too scornful and aloof for his own good. His magnetism was incompatible with the tribe's quiet unity, and Laus could already see how it drew all his wife's love rather than a lawful share of it.

Nomi told him he was going in to sleep, but was first getting warm by the fire. Laus murmured an acknowledgement.

The man wished they would venture from the clearing together, with Nomi's hand in his; wished they would return with shared pictures in their eyes, for the hill views were beautiful, the unpeopled landscape right for a growing boy to become strong in. But Nomi never moved from the clearing; would not go up and out into the bright air and stand next to his father. In that companionship was the stamp of an inheritance his purest self rejected.

Laus, aware of Nomi's reluctance, never invited him, just waited for the words, 'Let's go to the Eagle's Head, Papa'. Laus was steely with himself, woke early even in the winter cold, spoke little and never pushed the woman. But with the boy, steel became a solidity, an awkwardness.

"Mm," he grunted again and walked away. The boy frightened his spirit.

Nomi stayed, drawn to the flames. He wanted to lie down so the full heat could wrap over him and in its blanket he could relax. Relaxing meant leaving his body, letting it breathe on its own. He often went from it before sleeping, letting it sink into the floor bed, quiet, passive.

But tonight there was a new intensity in the little showdown with Laus and Ella that made Nomi want to lose himself *now,* to go this absolute moment. He needed Ella attracted, his father expectant, but at the same time he did not like the smell of their closeness. Pushing them away - which he often did when they turned to him with food in hands, clothes in arms, smiles on their faces - was not because he did not like them, it was because he did not want them. Unless he was hurt; unless the skin on his arm had been torn, as it had a day back, when running carelessly through the trees a branch had caught him. Then they had to be there, holding him, his cries searing the air, his head boring into their stomachs. It was a lover's game he played, which was why his mother had become hard and quiet.

Nomi stretched out by the fire, leaving his little building of sticks to be taken by the night wind. There were heaps of his things all over the clearing; games started and forgotten. Even his body sometimes looked as though it had been made carelessly, soon to be cast off.

"What are you doing Nomi?" Ella was back, bending over him and again close to his face. He opened his eyes. 'Almost circular,' she thought sometimes. 'His eyes are different from ours.'

"What are you doing?"

"Nothing," he said, though the experiences relaxation brought were spectacular; more important to him than the kindnesses these strong, brown people offered him; sweeter and more free.

It was a freedom, not just his but everyone's. It was everyone's slipping memory of better times that he was trying, in this sleepy oblivion, to secure, like stretching up to the white sky with a bird in his cupped hands, feeling the frightened beat of its wings against his palms.

Now she was pulling him back into being just Nomi, a caught child. And so he was cross without knowing why.

"Nothing."

A force field around him made her stand at a distance, though she broke it with harsh words. Anything to fetch him back. Her voice made his head throb.

"Come on Nomi. Game finished. Sleeptime."

"No."

"Yes!"

He got up reluctantly. She had spoilt his relaxation anyway. He could feel the defeat. She was baffled sometimes by his sudden retreat. Clever as she was with veins, organs, heart, trees, earth, wise about how to harness her physical strength and heal people with her hands, she had not grasped this pattern in her son.

She lay him down gently in the shelter. His little body was tired, for it hardly had the strength to carry these intense feelings, which sometimes had him bend to rub a toe caught at an odd angle, or put a hand to his spine when he should have been carelessly supple. Splayed out and limp, he lay on the leaves. But not for long. Activated by some force that was urging him up, his sleep was broken at three, his head tight and alert. An idea rattled his mind, a stone thrown into his soft dreaming: 'Go to the fire'. It relentlessly repeated itself until his legs untwisted and stretched into movement. His brain, almost absent from his anatomy, had no will.

Barely awake, he moved away from the humped bodies of his sleeping parents. Usually the ground, moving to his step, had Ella and the man sit up, alert. They had ears sensitive to disturbance, especially when it was their child. But their previous attentions to him had tired them out and they remained asleep.

He was ten or so inches from the fire, and in the suspension from reality where his dreams had taken him - dreams in which he saw a lit up earth; a memory of the womb, or maybe the womb the earth had been; a place where one remained a child, though the body grew up and around one like an expanding room into which people walked lightly without intruding, saw and appreciated one's possessions without wishing to possess, and instead added to them a gift, so that one felt constantly completed, not shattered by life - in that unreality, he walked to the fire, unaware of its danger.

Five inches now, for he was moving slowly, half asleep, his fingertips purposefully stretched towards the shimmering heat so they would become the light hands of his dream. He bent his knees to the compacted leaves, bringing his hands and face nearer to the ground, while his brown cheeks burnt in the darkness.

It was nice. He swayed his small face backwards and forwards. Yes, nice; like biting one's finger on and on to see how much hurting one can take.

Ella sat up. Maternally connected to the push and pull of Nomi's body, she felt the tug of heat on his hand. She did not scream. It was white heat she felt: silent, scorching, but it had her catapult like a leaping cat to snatch his middle and carry him bent in two to the ground they shared for sleeping.

She folded him into her, his dark head on her throat. And he slept there peacefully. The peace was a breaking of the hardness in him. He had frightened himself and when he was afraid he needed them.

The next morning, Laus, returning from his early morning climb, his face cold, water seeping from his eyes, was told by Ella what had happened. He was adamant, said they should put the fire out at night, that they should just keep each other warm. But Ella said no, Nomi would not do it again, he had learnt.

A week later - a week unspoilt by naughtiness, resistance, coldness; their bodies seeming to move more easily in tune with the tasks they carried out to tend their home - Nomi did it again. And again they slept. This time his fingertips touched the low flame. Just the tip, but enough to have him leap into the air, screech and recoil. Then they woke.

"Nomi, Nomi..." A torrent of protective reprimand: "Why, Nomi, why? Why do you keep doing this, you little devil?" It was only the second time, but the first had reverberated again and again in their heads. Now it was Laus who said there was no need to put out the fire because Nomi had burnt his hands.

After a third incident, they tied his hand with cloth, sat him between them, their energies combining in a canopy over him so that he felt trapped, and sternly demanded an explanation.

He started to cry. Not childish tears, but the dry, blank tears of one who just did not know. They were worried, sensing in the event an omen. Usually they did not have to think. They just saw life's quick causes and responded, but they experienced Nomi's perversity as an intrusion upon their peace, a resistance to life's fixed pattern. It made them fear for the future.

"What *is* it, Nomi?"

He kept crying.

"Fire-fly, fire-fly!" Ella teased him, changing tack, finding in herself the odd spark of humour which had once caught the eye of the Chief and made him reprove her with his eyes. But with Nomi it worked. It changed his mood sufficiently for him to listen and say sorry with bowed head.

For three years Nomi seemed to be all right. He still teased, but only with stones, with sleep, with food, not with fire. Only once did he test them. It was late and he was tired. Laus was preparing the shelter, and Ella had her back turned, looking for a moment into the navy sky.

Nomi picked up the cloth she used for wrapping food. Only for a few seconds were their backs turned, but long enough for Nomi to throw the cloth on to the fire, then run. Not far, but to a point where his father's long strides could not reach him, nor his mother's scream frighten him. He stood stiff, his hands smacked onto the bark of a tall larch.

Turning, they saw the flames flashing and twisting and, slipping inevitably into the thought he had laid for them, the flames were suddenly Nomi.

"It's him! It's him!" Ella clutched at Laus. Her arms, which earlier had curved fat and healing around a sick child, were straight and tense.

"It's Nomi!"

Laus was pinned by her so that he could not move closer to see. If they had reasoned, they would have known it could not be Nomi, for a body could not have burned so quickly, especially without a cry.

She screamed into the emptiness and Laus held her. A few moments later, Nomi appeared with a handful of leaves, makeshift flowers, and with awkward charm brought them to his mother.

It was Laus' turn to use humour, though he was not so good at it as Ella. He scooped up the leaves that had fallen through Ella's fingers and threw them in Nomi's face, chanting and teasing, keeping one hand on his woman's shoulder; protecting their cohesion with his arms. But there was a thread of anger tightening around the woman's brain.

Ordinariness resumed because to eat, sleep, love, was such an ingrained rhythm in their lives and Nomi was not brave enough to threaten it for long. He was sensitive to the language of eyes, and too often read suspicion in the sideward glances of the elders. Besides, a part of him liked to light the fire, to help cook, to sit peacefully into the evening. So a new phase began. He more frequently played with the other children, whose limbs tumbled with his in friendly fights, but never in the discomfort of intimacy. And they enjoyed being captured by his magnetism - it made their rock drawings seem more than mere scratchings; their running around more than just restlessness.

Laus was pleased to see him wander beyond the clearing, although still sad that they had never been out together. Nonetheless, he was satisfied that Nomi was developing a taste for tasks that would make him a good father. Certainly he was growing taller, his face broader and his bearing more solid. And watching his figure disappear into the trees one day as he left the clearing, Laus thought, 'He has a good back; a back that can work and carry on my line.' He went a little late to get wood because the process of transferring to his son, cell to cell, limb to limb, his own strength and shape had begun. He could afford to relax.

The handing over of power in this way was slow but visible, both in the gradual succumbing of child and the wide puckered brow of the Zuni Indian. But Nomi had been slower than most to absorb his inheritance, as if his bones wanted to keep their own shape. So when Laus saw this morning that the process had begun; that somewhere in the tight young body of his son an opening had come, joy filled his heart. And as the sun slipped like an orange penny out of the dark purse of the hills, he presented his face towards it to thank.

Outside the life of their clearing, a girl was growing beautiful. Her body knew that she was ready for marriage. There was nothing tangible to account for the change, but it was in her expression, the fall of her shoulders, her skin. And her hair, nourished as before, was drawing on something inside to thicken it. Nomi had known her all his life. She had been no more important than leaves, sticks, food. But now Imu was distinct, and he saw her in his sleep. True, Laus and Ella had put her there, their joint minds placing the image of marriage in his head, but he was receptive too, as not before.

When the dream had come several times, and when Nomi had seen the girl differently - his eyes turning to her face as they need not have done, for it meant purposely stopping to look - the words were spoken, the arrangements made for their meeting... Imu knew, Nomi knew, they all knew, and the Chief confirmed it, that it was the right time for them to unite.

The day was set for a year ahead. In the meantime, they remained as mere children, chewing skin off fruit, juice dripping down their satiny chins, shouting in voices that knew no innuendo.

On the morning of the wedding, his father painted him, bumping colour across his torso with his big hands. An energy filled the man and several times Nomi gasped at the hardness of his fingers. But the man persisted in a last effort to make the boy the strong form and colour he wanted him. It was a silent and solitary ritual. By custom no one was to see.

Ella was a little sick that day, maybe because she would lose her son, but also because there was a new seed growing inside her and it was breaking the rhythm of her breath.

When Nomi's body was fully decorated, they escorted him solemnly to dancing and love. Behind the calmness there was excitement, for the ceremony would be over quickly and after it the whole tribe would let go and forget time, duty and relationship with the elements - charming the sun, willing the rain - and dance, dance...

Imu was beside her father. Her skin was stretched tight across her high cheekbones and the parting in her raven hair seemed cut by a knife. As the men cheered and the women waved decorated branches, Laus and Ella led Nomi to her, stood him like a tree, and waited for the elder who would say the word for silence and for sound.

Some young boys, for whom the ceremony was a boring interlude before the fun, had lit a fire a few paces away. The solemnity made them wild, and they piled sticks fast to see if the flames could tower above them.

The elder put his hands on Nomi's arms. Through the colours on his face, his eyes looked distant. He hummed a few words, moved his hands over Nomi's body to bless his virility and then led him to the girl. They embraced. It was the first time Nomi had smelt the oil on a girl's neck or enjoyed the smoothness of skin other than his mother's.

He was transfixed by it and yet terrified; a terror more absolute than trepidation. He could not lie with this girl, not ever. And yet he wanted to touch her as he had the fire. Two voices raged in his head and one shouted louder.

Seconds later, the loudness became a scream that echoed around his pure body. He hurtled from this quiet spot of their joining; ran and ran, terrified by the will of his own body. He realised as he paused for breath that he was searching for a place to hide, for time to think. Though there had been days, weeks, months to ponder, it was this second that he needed to expand into a stillness.

He chose the clearing first, but even at a distance he saw that was not home any more. In less than an hour he had grown out of it. Then he thought of the Eagle's Head, but the climb was too long. He needed desperately the blankness of sleep or the darkness of a cave in which to forget and yet peacefully face the desires that rippled through his limbs. Puberty and marriage had overlapped without time for exploration or choice. So he had used force as one has to when laws are walls.

He wished for a real wall now; a solidity against which to lean and recover his breath. But there was nowhere. The community was an open space. All hearts known. Mother leant against father, child against ground, babe against breast. No one stood alone.

Nomi felt his tribe's anxiety stretch out to him as hands upon his body. They knew the danger of solitude, the threat of evil spirits and wanted him safe. Slow step after slow step, he walked back to the gathering, their collective thoughts disempowering him. Besides there was nowhere to go.

As he approached, he saw them straggling away like parts of a body shot to pieces. Laus. Ella. Their hurt reproduced itself inside him.

And Imu. Fleetingly he felt compassion as he watched her figure, still amidst the moving crowd. He might even have stretched out a hand, had her shock not created such a deep moat around her. Every atom of her body repelled consolation.

To steady himself, he touched one of the larch trees that bordered the marriage ground. He was within a child's stone throw of Laus and Ella. Again night fell inside him. Here was his tribe, whose sacred offering he had broken. He deserved to be turned on a spit.

Instead, the elder was walking towards him as if to scoop up a child who had fallen. His face was soft and forgiving. Nomi panicked. His arm lifted to hit the old man. No, not that Nomi! Don't do that! He stopped. Had he hit, the elder would have been forced to stand down: it was the custom that a single physical challenge to a holy man was a sign from the gods that he was unworthy. And more, Nomi would have been hemmed in by a curse.

But his fire-fly spirit needed freedom so badly. Bare, bright and fragrant as this landscape was, with its tall trees and green, untrodden valleys, it remained, for his rarefied self, too populated. He craved a silence that neither a submissive, organised life, nor a cursed life, would allow him. So he did not hit the elder and the elder did not know that his raised arm had carried the energy of violence.

Nomi would destroy himself instead.

As though to recover his composure, he walked to the fire which the boys had continued to stoke. Neither Ella nor Laus realised the purpose of his step. The running had humiliated them. This quiet walk was nothing.

At each step he thought, 'I don't want to come back to life again. I don't want it, I don't want it.' He knew the laws. Laus had lain beside him when he was small and explained in pictures about rebirth; had said, "So, Nomi, be good or you'll come back as a crow's child!" And the man had made his hands into a bird and, unafraid then, Nomi had laughed and thought, 'I'll be a crow's child...'

And now he did not want to come back as animal, as chief, as anything. Just to go. He begged over and over as he walked what seemed a great distance to the fire, 'Please... please... please... Just to go.'

Imu stood at a distance, but watching. Her face was iron hard. The humiliation had become too great for her brain to register. Instead it circled into her stomach as a virus that would break out later. Her father, who had witnessed the whole scene suddenly erupted. He had his bow and arrow ready. He would kill this young man who could not live by the rules of the tribe and who had insulted his daughter.

These were ruthless times; times when effect followed cause quickly and easily. The purity of its people meant punishment was harsh but infrequent. If a man stole, the animal slipped from his hunter's grip the next day and he went hungry; if he slept with the wrong woman he was maimed. It was a time and place without crime, for vengeance was contained automatically within its structure.

The weight and precision of justice was behind the father's square-ended fingers; made them rest gently in his palm as he prepared to use his bow. His eye was on Nomi's neck. And it was there, cleanly, like a swish of mountain air, that the arrow hit. The young man sank down, his face petrified, for the arrow had caught him at the exact moment when he had been falling forward to the fire. It spared him the sin of suicide.

As it was, the arrow, as tuned to the man's fingers as Nomi's will was to fate, shattered a fragment of his soul away. The hard, flint-like side of Nomi's mind that did not belong in a world of entanglements, separated itself. The rest of him was left to submit to the law. Away from the threat of involvement, it became soft, free, its own colours forming brightly in a darkness that was simply the absence of matter, as sleep is the absence of physical feeling.

Rehabilitated, unique again, it leapt absurdly, twinkled, flashed, then seared the sky. Here was that force, the earthbound form of which had been flirtation and mischief, but which had been so cramped, so fearful, for the tribe had been a safety net that caught joy before it became bliss, handsomeness before it became beauty. Away from that constriction, in a celebration different from arrogance for being unobserved, this minute, throbbing light had its day.

Everyone ran to dead Nomi in a panicking wave of colour. Only Ella was calm, for in the few moments after her son's death, a vital glow had filled her womb. Her mind was as shocked and terrified as theirs, but her body was placid and warm. And it was she who issued directions to the men to carry her son back to the clearing, leaving Laus, Imu's father and the elder in a triangle of tight anxiety under the evening sun.

SIRUS

The silver birch leans
in slender shade alone
when leaves fall
the harvest of his laughter
is gathered in by followers.

The rest of him was left to submit to the law...

Sirus put out his hand and imagined holding in it the robe, fully made; the abundant softness of its material swishing over his feet, the bumpiness of its embroidery and its neat seams, all finely gathered into a garment. Then he thought about the little tower of silver that would greet its completion.

He imagined putting the silver into the box in the cupboard, piling it next to the veil silver, the coat silver, the cloth silver. Sometimes he wished there were no silver; that he did not have to exchange for his work something round and flat that would buy more material to make more garments. These were circles he did not want.

What did he want? He did not know, except that it could not be fabricated, registered in an account book or written down (though what he received in return for this quiet, afternoon yearning, later had men in cold cells writing busily into the night). The trouble was, on the brink of a week in which another set of measurements would be noted down, another bargain made, he did not know what else to do. If he stopped, there was nothing.

Anyway, he had a mother, a father, a good home; could work outside with the warm sun on his bare head. He had sleep in the afternoons, good simple food, friends who came into his shop and broke the monotony with their chatter:

"Sirus, what are you making now...? What are you up to, eh?"

"Oh, just a coat," or, "Oh, just a veil," he would say.

Or Abra, his friend since childhood, would come by with, "Walk? Feel like a walk now? We'll only be out for an hour."

Then he would lean his long body back, stretch his neck, yawn and get up. And the two young men would wander into the warm afternoon, kicking and shuffling, relaxing themselves after a dusty morning humped over work benches. There was not much talk with Sirus, just the odd mumbling comment as a woman bent to pick up her child or a bird swooped low over the dry trees. But his body spoke. His dark body, in spite of his murmuring discontent, was harmonious and easy and made Abra like being with him. And Sirus, capable of forgetting an emotion before he had finished feeling it, would be lulled back to life.

Today was unusual. He felt a happy warmth unrelated to the promise of an afternoon off in the sun. A glow was building inside him, spilling out of his eyes and into the room. Abra, burly but sensitive, stooped to come through the door as if into a place for which he was too big and loud. Normally they chatted and chided each other in here; their words a careless part of the scraps of fallen cotton and aimless dust. Today, there was an awkwardness that drew them into quietness.

Leaving for the park, Abra took Sirus' hand. He felt the calluses on his friend's fingers, the dryness of his palm. Abra's chest hurt. Their friendship was coming to a close, but it would happen lightly like water seeping unseen into the ground. To stave off the change which they both sensed, they took the long route around the scrubby park, past the palm trees and azaleas.

Sirus soon forgot it; resumed his evening work with the same indifference as he had yesterday. The singsong of discontent, as routine as his breathing, broke out in mockery at the in and out of his needle: tomorrow someone will ask for an adjustment to a hem and someone else will try something on and then only when their fussiness has pushed us to the limit will they pay. And when he thought of the money, he felt tired; not as he might have done, pleased that it could buy another place to live, a change of town or job. He could not connect silver with new chances.

His mind stopped at the money so that he felt it was himself being totted up; his days piled one on top of the other, all the same size, the same shape, the same value. All his days strung together to make a new cooking place for his mother and a comfortable old age for his father who, Sirus had once worked out in a moment of boredom, must have missed the brilliant red sunset over fourteen thousand times while his head bowed over the work top.

He was about to leave that evening when a woman came into the shop to ask when her dress would be ready, how much it would cost and to pass the time, for she was a leisure woman, whereas he, pushed, lazy, dreaming, was not. He had to get on.

"Yes, fine," she said, but did not hurry out. Instead she stood in the small doorway looking at the pieces of material scattered around, considering whether to make another order, to start another cycle turning. Silent, he did not encourage it. His dark head bent to resume work, and she said, "Maybe not," and left him alone.

Sirus sat inert in the workroom. The boredom which he had felt earlier became a peaceful emptiness and he found it hard to form another thought about moving. He neither wanted to stay nor go. Nothing in the room seemed connected with him. He had scanned the shelves a thousand times, knew every grain of their wood, had searched the floor for fallen material, mended the legs of the work bench. The room was imprinted on him. But the peace, a part of the afternoon's glow, was wiping him and this place clean of each other.

He lay his head on the work bench. His body felt light and relaxed; absent almost. He began to sense that he was waiting for something; began to know it, as if it had happened before and he just had to pace through it again: his hand had lit that candle before, his eyes had turned to the door before. He made few movements, and knew every one of them in advance. It was pleasant, like being an observer of himself, and it took his mind into a deeper peacefulness which made the room feel as sacred as it had to the casual body of his friend. It was a feeling that echoed the way the religious men did things: slowly, sparsely.

He shifted a little. The move broke the quietness and made him heavy against a wash of lightness. Then again stillness, closed eyes, soft lids over black orbs. What was it? Behind the lids a blue, a purple, a red. He was absorbed by the colours. The room disappeared. Only barking dogs anchored his existence as, somewhere in the distance, they called around corners and gathered to ravage some pile of discarded food.

A thought rose to the surface about going home. He sensed his mother seated, waiting and sleepily wondering where he was. But the thought sank back into the softness again. Another tried, failed and fell apart. Nothing could touch him. Had it not been for this drowsiness, he would have been afraid, for he was entering a nothingness too strong to return from.

The flame he had lit flickered in the breeze that was coming through the door. He opened his eyes to watch it: those dark eyes that would later haunt soldiers ordered to hurt him. They were mild eyes now. They had not yet loved; had turned towards one or two women with feeling, but not seriously. There had always been a blandness in those he might have chosen, so instead he immersed himself in work. He had stayed gentle, and was gentler still now, in the candle light.

What he was waiting for hovered with the peaceful control of one who knows the right moment to enter. Without senses it could not watch nor listen for its cue; could only move by instinct like a flower opening to the sun. Folded and quiet for centuries, it expanded into an impulse too strong to be retained in that quietness; shifted minutely in its own light world, intensified, propelled itself outwards and away from the warm shell in which it nestled. It, that would later digest and walk, love and reject like everyone else, was still hardly human. It, that had mapped across its mind a whole picture of message-giving and confrontation, was as unchallenging now as a dust particle or seed floating downwards.

Why Sirus? Why did this messenger choose a casual tailor whose brain embraced nothing more than the immediate concerns of life - eating, sleeping, walking? Why not a pharaoh, a pharisee, a landowner, someone whose material power could publicise its arrival? Because they were representative of the times. Their misguided ambitions were like arrows rebounding merely on the small target of their own lives. Sirus had no ambition, no ties, and an emptiness so great that it could accommodate the extraordinary far-reaching power of a messenger.

Sirus did not know, carelessly dropping the material on the floor, what had happened; did not know that as he moved another being also moved; had slid deeply into the softer parts of his mind: the parts which were not concerned with his work and yet into which he himself had lately been drawn. His mother had noticed this distancing, but there was something virginal about her which kept her from prying. When he had silently urged the customers away, sought a little more space and as now stayed late to work, it had been his preparation; like when a person enters a room unused for a long time and cleans the grate, lights a fire, dusts, gets ready for a guest. Sirus had been experiencing the pleasure of anticipation and yet also the forlornness of finding himself so devoid of passion.

He got up. He should have been tired as he walked the road he had walked every day for twelve years - usually beside his father, even at thirty, for they were friends and it was discussing time at night. His limbs were relaxed as if already rested, but apart from that everything was ordinary. And the silence of the next morning was ordinary too, and his father's sleepy chiding was ordinary, though curiosity made the man ask again, "Where were you, Sirus?"

"At the shop."

"So late?"

"To finish something."

So vague? Sirus quite businesslike usually. 'He's still half asleep,' his father thought.

"Who for?"

Sirus sat up.

"I had to stay," he said. His directness satisfied his father, but underneath, the man was troubled. A fear was rising in him. More than once in the past few months, a memory had come to him like a feather floating upwards which he could not quite catch; a memory of loss, of a dark patch.

Sirus still did not know that his mild mind had pulled into itself another; had no idea that this influence, now so imperceptible, would have him leave the shop, leave his home and speak on hills about things he had never seriously considered before (why should he?); about why it is wrong to cheat, about how to make a feast out of what looks dry and meagre. He just greeted his family as usual, ate in the room in which he had always eaten - dusty, goat smelling, warm - the food he had always eaten - bread, cheese, milk; the family's heads bent over the table, a foursome unbroken.

After breakfast, he remembered the material left on the floor. Today he would finish that work. He would work hard all day. He felt energetic and simple. When they arrived, his father picked up the material that lay discarded.

"Sirus," he chided, "that's not good workmanship."

"It fell father. It was late. I was tired."

Again the question. Why had he not come home earlier then? And besides, look how little had been done in all those hours. Only one seam as far as his father could see.

"No, two," Sirus pointed out, "two." The day began to fray. The messenger inside withdrew from everyday carelessnesses and Sirus felt dry again, as if he had woken to an occasion that was really on another day. But it was not just an ordinary day because Sirus noticed for the first time that his father was strained. He saw the lines on the man's face. Maybe he too felt the burden of the circles; maybe his father struggled sometimes; maybe Abra did; maybe... The world opened up a little and Sirus saw beyond himself.

"Come on Sirus, it doesn't matter. As long as we finish it today, the woman will be satisfied with her purchase." Sirus was comforted by his father's sternness, behind which the man concealed his difficulty with remembering his customers' names. Sirus put his head down and worked. They stayed quiet and the atmosphere re-settled with the rhythm of the work so familiar and comfortable.

In the settledness, his silent visitor expanded into thought. It had never had a thought before; had reached Sirus, as one moves thirstily towards water. But now it was going to drink, to draw on the facility it had found, and produce an idea. And the idea registered in Sirus' brain as he sewed. He had been thinking about lots of things, but this thought was distinct. It linked him with last night, with the gutted candle and the silence. He looked at the melted wax on the sill and in his looking the thought came again, more strongly and clearly as his friend enjoyed his first drink: 'Today go out alone - to a private place.'

And because this dual control had to start easily and without burden, Abra, whose feet were bound almost daily for Sirus since childhood, decided against him in favour of sleep. He too had rested little the night before, alone, separate, tossing and hot. And because a little tug of doubt threatened Sirus' obedience to this vicarious direction - he never walked alone - his father, also tired, told Sirus he would go home for a few hours to rest. The doubt faded.

Sirus walked fast and purposefully, free for the first time of an ingrained laziness that he and Abra had shared. He arrived at a mound, nothing special, but he wanted to stop there. He sat for a few moments on the brown grass with his arms around his knees, then relaxed, stretched out, closed his eyes and lightly dozed. And in the haziness images shimmered in front of his closed eyes. A boat tossed; a thin figure walked through the sand, a woman pulled at his clothes. He tried to hold on to them, but they slipped past as only signals, trusting him to take their fragrance fast.

As they faded, an actual woman walked past, balancing a pitcher of water on her head. She saw Sirus lying quiet, his eyes closed, ostensibly only a young man resting after a morning's work. But observing him, a fear shifted from her mind. Sirus did not know she was there. The energy emitted by the gentle intertwining of the two beings inside Sirus' dark head made other people open and relax too. Even the most intolerable possibilities became bearable. And Sirus himself could have been told: 'Sirus you will have your arms torn from their sockets,' and at that moment he would have felt only love...

Not knowing that this being would knock down great walls, he welcomed him in. And what had been monotonous routine became delightful. Eating, for instance. His guest had never tasted sweet bread crumbling in the mouth, the hot gurgle of milk around the slippery path of the throat. It had felt the sleepiness of the huge vault of light around it, but never the sleepiness of a full stomach. Sirus began to savour life.

"Sirus, why are you walking so slowly?" his father asked one day.

"Dunno."

"Come on, boy." The man a little frustrated. For, as he was getting older, he relied on the young man to be the quick, efficient hands and feet of his business. But it was the feel of the foot on stone; the solidity, the smoothness. It was so very nice. The guest liked it. Liked too the ease with which it could withdraw from the feet and just be itself again while the legs would continue walking.

The next stage was change, at a pace so fast that sometimes Sirus had to sit quietly, head in his hands, to steady himself. The guest assumed residence, started rearranging Sirus' mind. Previous affections fell away and the effort of his work routine became almost intolerable.

One day he found himself telling his father that he was leaving home. The man said nothing until a week later, a mountain of material on his workbench, he turned to Sirus, tears welling in his eyes, and pleaded with him. Sirus wished he could feel pain. He understood pain. But instead there was a blankness so deadening that he almost filled it with a recapitulation. The words formed ready but then Abra came in and filled the blankness for him, his large feet shuffling across the dusty floor like fate whispering.

"Sir," he began. "I'm sorry, but..."

"What?" the old tailor snapped.

The boy explained he had lost his job, that business had failed, that he was wondering if the old man could put up with his clumsiness; whether he might consider employing him.

Sirus froze at his workbench, his head tightening with excitement at the signal his friend's offer provided. If Abra came, Sirus could go. Three days later he went. Nowhere in particular. Just wandered like a prisoner drinking his freedom deeply. When he stopped at a place, it was because he was told to. In the stretches of silence as he walked, he learned to listen to instructions. They came crudely as from one for whom language was alien. Stay here... eat this... sleep now.

Sometimes the messages came through his eyes. He found himself gazing at a man as though calling him and the man came to him asking the way to the market place; his soul meant to salvation. He became Sirus' first follower and after that they were as inseparable as a king and his bodyguard.

More came. They brought with them skills and provisions which made their nomadic life easy. Sometimes when they settled at night, Sirus would tell stories. The words were simple but inside them messages nestled like hidden gifts which reached each listener differently. There was the excitement of youth and revolution in the air though many of those who huddled on the hillsides were old and ordinary.

Amongst them was a woman. She had black hair, a face made of the same softness as Sirus' own. He felt drawn to her with the confidence of one who has newly found his own attractiveness. One night, while the others slept, he went to her in the darkness, felt her body nestle into his. They stayed there for a few moments, each able to hear the other's desire. It was a moment of bliss in which the fullness of his own mind balanced perfectly with the prospect of filling this woman with his seed.

But then suddenly a rock tumbled down the hillside and hit the man who had sought the marketplace. He sat up alert and saw Sirus, usually so straight, separate, as a double form in the darkness. Sirus scrambled up. The man's body looked like the mountain. A power had entered it and Sirus knew he could not have the woman.

The next day, he withdrew into himself and walked alone to restore his coolness. And the woman he had wanted, withdrew the thread that joined them, wound it round her fingers and made cloth for the wall hangings in the temple. For sensual as she was, the spirit in Sirus had touched and awakened her purity.

The shock made him careful, made him widen the gap between his inner life and the applause it won. A new level of clarity came and the silent cupping of these two minds made the sound of Sirus' words stretch. Even the priests came and listened though they did not leave their posts. Instead grabbed for more wine, money, acclaim. It was a response at least, which is what stunning lovers always win, even if it is only a turn of the head.

And the intensity of Sirus' involvement, the more total for being without the barrier of a body, made his hands seem significant as they gestured, his face subtle as he spoke. He was alone, sparse, quiet, but the feeling he radiated was of being cherished.

It was not always easy. Sometimes the power behind him would withdraw just when it was needed. Once Sirus had gathered a whole crowd around him. The tolling bell had made them drop what they were doing and come quickly. A woman had patches of flour on her arms, a man led a ragged goat by the ears, others looked dishevelled and interrupted. But they were there, for when the bell tolled, one came.

Sirus stood, a pillar in the middle of a wave of colour and gossip. He started to speak. There had been a rumour. It had to be stopped. Faith. Silence. Determination. The words did not need sentences. Faith. Usually when he said it, feet shifted, minds pictured standing calm at the forefront of an army. But today, because for some reason the guest was sitting well back in Sirus' head, giving the words he spoke no resonance, faith became an ominous building, a place to be fled. The people stayed on the hilltop listening, but their minds went back home.

That was how it was at the end, when the guest who had lived in him for three years departed. It had come, delivered its messages and gone, leaving Sirus behind, fragile as a lover who has given too much. His mind was a garden of flowers, but in his heart, where the guest had been was darkness: a black hole into which unsuspecting friends would, lives later, fall in love, hatred, simple attraction.

And on the last day, reduced, skeletal, his mind a grey rock in a tomb body, only then did he hover on the edge of truth: the horrible realisation that he had been inhabited not inspired. People would speak of him as the tailor who became a storyteller and he alone would know the unrelatedness of the two. It was a devastating moment of abandonment, followed by a blankness with which he was deeply familiar.

He saw before him an eternity of loneliness, of being congratulated for what he had not done. And the love that had been a power in him, strong enough to transform the most mundane and cynical of minds, switched in one second to a fire of unforgiving anger. His body, already in pain, raged as it received the impact of this thought: that he had been betrayed by someone whom he had trusted so completely that he had entrusted his own mind. Their two lines of thought had become one wide road for others to walk. And now he was a single, hairline track going nowhere. Though he was dying by the hands of other people, it was his own anger that might well have been the death of him...

But for his father's face.

The man had walked all the way to the prison where Sirus lay, to witness the death he had already experienced when Sirus had left home. The double sorrow was almost too much for his frame to bear.

And when, between the moving forms of leather-bound soldiers, Sirus saw that face, he saw how far he himself had come in the three years that had separated them. It was a stark and sudden reminder of an exquisiteness to which he had become too accustomed. He felt a deep compassion for the pain in his father's face, but at the same time his spirit soared with the knowledge of its own gain. He had moved from subservience to leadership - or so he thought. And the old man, made sensitive by loss, rose on the energy of Sirus' discovery, above the prospect of his son's death.

He left before the end. Went home, carrying a fragment of hope in his hands which he, like the woman on the hillside, turned into lengths of crimson cloth for a robe.

CORINA

*I have been stood in this wood
for so long
thought the poplar on a hot day.*

He had moved from subservience to leadership - or so he thought...

Corina sat waiting for her sons to arrive in a room that was warm and prepared. There was nothing physically different about the place, no special decoration, lacy runners or bottle of wine on the table, except that the pots on the stove were fuller than they had been for some time. But she had shaped the atmosphere like a womb, made it potent and inviting, and having finished her work, she had time for a smoke. It was her favourite few moments as the soft pungent tobacco, circling down into her system, slowed and relaxed her.

Once here, the men, with their large unwieldy bodies, would break the silence and dirty the floor with their boots. Not that she minded; she loved them, and a mother makes a home to be unmade. But it was pleasant to sit in her creation for a while and anticipate them.

Her ankleless legs rested on the white stool in front of her and she looked at them as though they belonged to someone else, wondering how they had come to be so fat. Had they grown gradually without her noticing? Her own flesh, and she not seen? They were unstockinged; she did not like the feel of material on her limbs and always worked bare-armed and legged, even in the cold, while other women cloaked themselves in black.

All the women in the village had fat legs, while their men had spindly limbs under baggy cloth pants and lying in wooden beds were frequently breathless not from desire but from the sheer weight of their wives. They ate double, but their energy went into the angry anxiety of making ends meet as they yanked at tangled nets and shouted to each other across high winds.

Corina's legs did not bother her. In fact she had only thought about them today because they were in front of her. She had no need to worry about her body. It was irrelevant to the love that drew her sons away from their boats, every late spring, for her birthday.

Seeing her at rest, lying on her low bedding that overlooked the west of the island with its white foam beating onto pale sand, one would only have given a passing glance, for she was like any other old woman in the village, a shade uglier even. Little hairs, resistant to makeshift tweezers, sprouted on her chin and the flesh on her arms wobbled as she turned to scratch herself. But seeing her awake, it was clear what drew them. She lived life carefully. Even laying out the mats on the stone floor had a particular bend and stretch, a particular movement of her palm to the small of her back, a particular moan as she straightened. And the moan became a gentle dip in the silence; a place to rest in. Mid-morning saw her seated on the step outside in the sun, and at twelve-thirty the hand would go to the spine again and she would be up and in, busy preparing. One knew where to find her and how she would be, and that was a comfort both to sons at a distance and to the disengaged part of her personality which, when its moment came, would need steady ground on which to land.

When her husband used to come home, lugging his body through the door as though he wished to be free of it, or to live in the warmth of hers instead, she would always come to him happily, and would wait to bring his food until he was seated and ready, knowing to the second when his legs had eased and the muscles in his stomach were loosened ready to receive her offering.

After his meal they would embrace. If the day's catch had been a good one he would laughingly lift her into the air. And the lift was the catch; the hat on the hook thrown or placed was the mood of the crew; the number of helpings eaten the sales made. The day he refused her thick soup, pushed it away angrily, she knew the winter ahead would be a hard one. In fact it had killed him. He was too old to captain the boat, too stubborn to leave it and he paid for it.

Corina had kept the fire going after he had died. And she still had power enough to pull her sons, for it had been stoked over years and had a beauty which her pretty daughters-in-law lacked. In fact she had power over the whole village. They liked her. She knew how to face life, to make it round and strong when its shape became like the long, knotted sticks they collected from the hillside for firewood. She was brave.

Sometimes in the winter the tide would rise very high and wash away parts of the sea wall. Once some of the houses in the harbour had gone too, shifting and tilting in the wind, then pausing as though suspended in mid-air before finally toppling into the water. For days, broken bits of furniture had floated on the soon calm water, while the women's minds remained rough and troubled. And ever since, whenever a storm brewed, they would make their ark in one house. It was not Corina's house, but when she came through the door, late usually because she thought they were fools to be afraid, they used her derision as reassurance and relaxed.

Had she lived now, travelled through time protected, carrying undiminished that private force, she might have been an actress. For it was an actress's power she had: to destroy everyone else's conversation and have them all turn and listen. She would have had that quality that makes a director risk his credibility and choose a woman because she has a quality other than beauty; a rough elegance which if fashioned carefully could make her a winner. She was a star without a context, and the villagers silently chose her as the centre of their village.

"Mama!"

The solitude was over. They came together, bending their large heads through the doorway. It was the only time they walked together. She did not know why, but somewhere, sometime back, her boys had fallen out. Over money, she thought. But Corina chose not to see that and greeted them as brothers as well as sons.

"Mama!" Spiros, the youngest, hugged her, held her at arm's length and looked into her yellow face.

"You look well," he said, then lifted her up, fat legs now six swinging inches from the floor. He laughed close to her face. Her nose not her mind registered the smell of wine, for she was occupied with the nice feeling of hands on her middle and was enjoying the memories it brought. He sang a Greek song as though to his love and plonked her back in her chair. The two other men were more reserved and kissed her on both cheeks as she sat.

She was pleased having the boys close to her flesh, giving her presents: a lace square for her chair, a sharp knife, an embroidered picture imported from Italy and bought in the market.

And she was glad none of the three was unmanly; glad that none of them had joined the flourishing Greek Church, donned tall black hats and become holy. Her senses would have withered at that, though she had her religion. The house was her sanctuary, and leaving it to be with the other women of the village, or to fetch in grains or vegetables to store in the dark room off the kitchen, she was always glad to be back. The air inside her home was the only air in which she could really breathe.

She did not mind that she hardly went out, or indeed, that she had never left the island - not once; had never visited her sons' homes, seen their wives or her grandchildren anywhere but here. Though her mind pictured accurately their bodies fishing, lugging in nets, bartering, pulling off their boots in the white-washed entrances of their houses. It was a talent she, had mentally to enter and influence their lives. She had almost as much control over the salty dampness of Spiros' boat as over her own cooking pots; her existence a carousel of images of which her own tidy little cottage was only one.

"What's cooking, Mama?" Spiros asked as he had done a thousand times as a child coming in from some rough game. He had always hurled himself about. 'He'll show them on the mainland how to live, my boy will. None of this lying and cheating. He'll be a brother to them.' Then he would come in through the door like a hungry little animal and she would praise him too much and afterwards be cross with herself and give him less cheese. 'If my boy's to be good, I'll be strict with him.' But he would steal into the little stone room at the back of the kitchen and cram meat into his mouth and run off gnawing. She knew he did it, but her attachment to him blinded her.

Now she laughed and went to stir the pot. She knew what to do to make him a child again. She knew which apron to wear, which dish to cook. She knew, as she knew many things about their life on the mainland, that their wives made moussaka, but it was not as good as hers. She knew that the quality of the tomatoes was good there, but that their pots were too new and they burned. Their arms were pink and young as they stirred but there were children pulling at them. When Corina cooked, her whole mind went into it.

As a child, eating had quietened Spiros down. "More, more," he had said then, and he did the same now, stretching the plate towards her from his big knees that had spent the week rubbing against the bottom of his boat. It had been a hard few days and the prospect of Sunday had run guiltily through him as he struggled to maintain his business.

He was beginning to be a liar, and being a good man it made his body tense. It had started with small mistakes: giving the wrong change, then missing out figures in his accounts. Last week he had lied in words, his voice boldly telling a man that the fish he had ordered had already been delivered, that if it had not arrived it must have been stolen. Then he had flapped his bag up and down against his stomach as if to show the man it was empty and walked away, for inside the bag was the cold slab of fish they spoke of. He could have admitted his mistake so easily, but the man's nose annoyed him, as his wife's did, and so he lashed out. He never lashed out at his wife so he lied to the customer instead. And when the customer left, Spiros had thought of Corina and Sunday and he stretched out to her as to a lifeline.

After the meal, Corina sat thinking about the leaking pipe and broken gutter. Spiros heard it; he in his way was her lifeline too:

"Anything you need fixing, Mama?"

She professed surprise, though inside she sung that she was still able to speak to him in thoughts.

It had always been Spiros. As the youngest child, it had been he who had stayed with her while the other two went fishing; he who had walked behind her past the whitewashed huts, down the path, scrub on either side, just heat and blueness above and below; he who had slid into the clean turquoise water with her and dived, his feet kicking into the island air.

The other two had been trained for work, but Spiros understood pleasure. The holding of a squirmy sea animal between finger and thumb, the throwing of it at his mother's face, not wanting to hurt but to try all feelings, all touches, all colours. And Corina, herself a shell shaped by the swell of her boy's affections, enjoyed these little pleasures because they were his.

Once they had climbed out of the water, their two bodies dripping and aching and had sat to dry on the hard slab of rock where they had left their clothes. Their skin was the same colour, the same wetness, the veins and organs in their bodies flawed in the same way and they had just lain there as one. Spiros had started to babble excitedly about a boat coming. She had sat up and seen the boat too and wondered why he was concerned. Then, briskly he had dived into the water and started swimming, turning to shout at her that he would reach the boat by sunset. She had shouted at him to come back, that it was too far, but he had laughed and carried on, his strong little body racing through the water, as if it were only yards he had to swim not miles. His eyes were still young and they had seen the boat as closer than it was; thought it was his father's boat. Swimming fast, he had soon tired and started floating on his back. And she, having dived to follow him, caught him up and explained distance to him as he clung onto her neck. He had cried because somehow that illusion broken was a thousand other things broken too: abilities that were merged inside him as memories of being able to touch and smell and hold feelings more subtle than those this seascape with its dark rocks could ever arouse.

They had swum back to the slab and she had fed him white cheese and fruit, knowing the depth of his disappointment. She too had felt it so many times; had felt the emptiness that follows a dream broken or a departure from intimacy. She had filled that space in herself with children and food - a respite, at least, from the blankness of her real state. And now, in the same way, she encouraged Spiros to eat.

When they were back home, their bodies relaxed and tired, they had lit a fire to welcome the others. It became a secret: "Please Mama, promise you won't tell them that I couldn't swim very far!" And he had held her wrist, scrunching her veins, until he was certain that she would not make fun of him. Part of it was that he wanted a secret with her and part of it was that he was ashamed that he had a mind that was less logical than his father's.

It had been a childhood that had lasted for an age; had been filled with a lightness that carried the burden of poverty easily. There had never been a sense of having too little. The house was small, but Corina was big and everything she touched was big; her spoons bigger, her pots bigger than the other women's. And the heavy cotton skirt that she wore somehow fell well and made her in those young days seem beautiful, though her features were ordinary. Pain circled outwards and away when she was there, and her husband looked at her nightly, knowing that he was lucky, very lucky, and that it was her strength that moved his arms in and out of the boat so constantly when the other men were ailing. But she would not hear of it. When he was romantic, told her in the night that she was his life, she guffawed and would not utter her love in words; as if she remembered the danger in public declarations of feeling. Instead she put her love into domestic activity.

She knew how to place the clothes ready, when to say, 'Now to bed.' And she also knew, to the finest extent, how to withdraw; when to say, 'Go on then, go. Do what you want.' So many times, those boys had come to her for consolation and she had said, 'No Andreas, no,' and pretended to be disinterested. And he had come back again and again and asked, 'Please, please, please,' for he as well as Spiros, though more quietly, was reliant on her strength.

But they heard very little now. Life had caught them and they stopped feeling her, except Spiros whose incomplete love for his wife left space for Corina.

Often she called to him across the water and indistinctly he heard her. But when he was in front of her, her needs reached him as items on a list: the gutter, the pipe.

And now he had finished, done what she had silently asked, he sat alone with her in the growing darkness. Stathis and Andreas slept. Corina took the chance to enquire about his wife.

"Is she well Spiros?" Able in her request to light up the woman and sustain her son's marriage, she cunningly did the opposite, for she was afraid of losing him.

"She is good," Spiros said, which she was, though there was no fire.

He pictured his woman. Nose apart, she was handsome and he felt the strength of her long brown body as he spoke of her, but it was a cold vase into which he could pour nothing more potent than the cool water of affection. His mind was not aware of it, but his feet knew as they walked up the hill each year, that he had come to get Corina's fire instead. Most of it was in the food, but a little came also between the words spoken as the other two snored in their chairs.

After the party was over, the men, heavy with food, got up to leave. Spiros sensed, as he moved to the door, that both his body and mind were changed. He felt he had been away from the frayed ends of his life for a week and now he could pick them up again with stronger fingers. Andreas' departure too was a happy one. Refreshed by the rest, he stretched, and Corina, alert to the messages on half-asleep faces - her husband's waking frown had told her well before time that he was to die before her - saw that Andreas was afraid of his own nastiness. He had made a gash in a man's chest three weeks before and had been devastated. It had happened quickly, with no hatred, just tiredness. But then he had done it again, differently, to his wife. And sometimes when he woke in the night, he thought that he might be a little mad, that a pattern was forming which might lay itself over his life. She touched his coarse-shirted arm, as she had when he had hit as a child and was flailing about saying, "It was him, not me." There was stability in her hand.

He joined Spiros and they walked in step. Stathis was a gentle man. Corina felt distant from him, but her hand clutched his arm too as they hugged good-bye. His body suddenly felt potent.

When they had gone, Corina felt drained and sat down, deciding to leave the clearing up until later. Tomorrow would do. She wanted to sit forever. But spurred on by a need for resolution, she got up again to tidy the room.

She recognised this sensation: 'If I had to speak now for more than one minute, my words would lose themselves between brain and mouth.' Her heart felt tight. Something made her go on with the plates. 'Just two more. Just the pans now, Corina. Just the cupboard closed. Whoop! Up with those arms! Then you can rest.'

Distant, faintly humorous, she was danced forwards, puppeted to finish her work by an absent master who required completion. In its world, a small oversight was a whole life lost, a whole army defeated. And following the woman's destiny as part of its own, it momentarily allowed her no compromise.

It was her sons' departure that weakened her. Though it was she who had provided fire, their bodies, winding down the hillside path until they were tiny dots on the white sand, had drained the strength from her twisted veins. Somewhere far inside a warmth and a pain mixed; a pressure that had been building broke. She sat down quickly and rested her head on her lap. So often her sons had found comfort there. And now - she dying - they knew nothing; were quiet and content, rowing the boat home on the lit-up water.

She lifted herself up onto the bedding, pretending she could not feel the strange warmth of blood in the wrong place. She put her hand on her heart. It had always worked before, had quietened the fast beat. But the warmth became a heat and she knew something was fatally wrong.

Her fat legs seemed to join as one as she lay observing the ebb. They were stronger as one and helped to distract her from the ache in her chest. She knew the blood was watery; had seen it when she had spat a little on the edge of a knife, when it had mingled in two tiny rivulets with the blood of a fish she was gutting. It had been too red, too thin. Maybe that was why it had escaped into the wrong place.

There was nothing she could do. The women in the village would be sleeping.

'It'll be all right,' she growled to herself as she had done to the boys when they fell down on the dark rocks of the island beaches. 'Just lie still.'

Corina was gone. She was not in their nets any more. And there was no hill walk to see her.

It was a bad first few months. The pattern emerged fully in Andreas. His wife was frightened by the way he moved in the house. He seemed to want to hurt her. And he found ways of doing it that were as clever as his mother's ways of helping had been. He would leave possessions in design for his wife's feet to stumble over. She was tired and her feet stumbled easily.

Spiros also shook a little. A few more lies, a woman, a fishing boat sunk; the hole in the wood as small but lethal as the one that made his mother's heart fail, and his too when he lost her.

Stathis' life seemed to take a turn for the better. His wife had their first child, and its face was as perfect and bronzed as they could have hoped. Except that it did not open its eyes for several days. They kept looking and looking, touching the lids coaxingly like worshippers of an idol they longed to come alive. Try as they might, they could not continue their chores for long without being drawn back to the side of the cradle.

A few days after the birth, they invited Spiros and Andreas to their house for a celebration. The old hurts were absorbed by the birth. It seemed undignified to fight in front of this tiny goddess. They cleaned the house, bought special wine, laid out bread and slabs of cheese and prepared for a party. There were a dozen or so guests and they sang and danced that evening as they had not since their wedding ten years ago. And all the while that their legs and arms swung up and down in unison, the child lay still, her silent power at the centre of their happiness.

Every now and then Stathis would disentangle himself from the music, the laughter, the wine, and slip into the bedroom to look, for there lay not just his child but his virility. He felt a strange ecstasy as he watched the little one and heard at the same time the sound of banging feet in the next room. And here only stillness; the peace that surrounds a mind devoid of thought, like paper upon which others would draw. This child would be made; not make itself.

In the darkness, he could half see the piles of white towelling placed by his wife, the jars of cream; her altar to motherhood. And impulsively he wanted his wife there with him, for it had been her struggle this creation; she, whose skin was torn so that this would be their only child and maybe the end of their physical love. He had tried to forget this fact in the rosy days after the birth because it frightened him. But standing here in front of his child, he felt calm and resolved: what he had sought from their nightly tumbles was compensated for by this child. He picked up his baby and touched, with his square fingertips, the parchment skin of its brow.

Sensing his touch upon her child, his wife slipped away from the party to join him. And it was she who noticed in the darkness a shine that was more than the reflection of the fingernail moon through the window; was the shine of eyes.

Stathis noticed the stiffness in his wife's body. Alert as a man hitting on a shoal of leaping fins in the dark water, he knew by instinct when the thing waited for has happened - sometimes the fishermen would sit up all night in their boats, heavy with sleep, their nets empty, when a sudden heaviness, a tug made them as alert and light as athletes moving their arms and shouting to each other.

"What is it?" he whispered.

"She's opened her eyes! Look, look, her eyes!"

Stathis relaxed, and his big hands went around the child and he lifted her into the air, swinging her up to the ceiling, her little fat legs dangling out of the lumpy sculpture of towels, and then back down to his wide chest which suddenly felt tight with terror. Their faces were close now and the baby started to cry. His heart was thumping as he handed the child back to its mother.

Those eyes, which had opened into the darkness were eyes he knew. Oh yes, he knew them; as if they had been a part of him for a lifetime.

Never before had Stathis' presence been missed. He was not a magnet. But as he returned to the party, there was a pause in the guests' dancing, and their energy came to him in a welcoming wave of affection.

He danced exuberantly, then out of breath from a high-kicking spin, too much for him after the shock of seeing his child stare at him with his mother's eyes, he slumped against the wall. His wife came to him, carrying the baby in her arms. Filled with a multitude of shifting feelings, he snatched the child from her, hugging it tight - she warning him a little of a baby's fragility. A flood of tenderness filled him; a tenderness of which his own babyhood and childhood had been devoid.

And when Andreas joined them, he sensed the change in their mood as only one who has touched the edge of madness can do. He told them that Spiros had left about twenty minutes before, looking upset. Stathis put his departure down to the drink and forgot him.

Andreas stayed, aware in some obscure way that this party had been, for his brothers, the funeral party they had never had. It didn't surprise him that Spiros had stormed out. He sat down heavily on the kitchen stool, his mind a grey cloud after the exertion of touching the pulse of the scene. Steadying himself with his large hands on the stone worktop, he watched the baby being lifted again and again into the air. It seemed in its tinyness very vulnerable, like someone old. His hand went to the wine bottle at his side.

PIERRE

The wilful willow wanted to be water
so the river gently bent her
and made the wish graceful.

And here only stillness; the peace that surrounds a mind devoid of thought, like paper upon which others would draw. This child would be made; not make itself...

It was only a river, but Pierre was there with it every morning before the family ate. He had invested in it all his feelings and it filled a part of him that was free and empty; a part which even the most affectionate of human gestures had no power to touch.

"Where is he?" asked Marie, his mother, weary of knowing the answer and wishing that Catherine would say, 'Playing with Gaston or Phillipe,' hoping that maybe, looking out of the narrow window, she would see him dashing in and out, strong-bodied and laughing.

"He's at the river."

"Ahh," his mother sighed.

"Mmmm..." concluded Catherine.

"Tchhh," his mother again.

It was a conversation so familiar that it could be had in a turn of the body, bang of the jug on the table or, as today, in tired whimpers. They never took it far into words, for words would stamp it with an aberration their sensitive minds dare not consider. And when Pierre came through the door, glowing as if he had been with a lover, they would busy themselves and wait for the request for food which would bring him back into a realm of which they were in charge.

And he conformed to their expectation, for it was safer and easier to snap back into ordinariness; to let go of everything precious rather than try to shape it to suit their questions. And this is why he lied to them. He wasn't a bad boy.

"Maman, I am hungry," he would say, and in seconds it would be in front of him: bread, cheese, jam. And he would eat fast and thoughtlessly so that it sat inside him, undigested. It was they not he who needed the food. His nourishment was the twist and turn of water, not the solidity of starch. He was made of movement and crystal swirls of sparkling green, blue...

Pierre went to the river because it inspired him to paint. It ran through his head as colour, form and image so that he became it, and the paintings that followed were simply extensions of its feeling in his body: the blues his calmness, his flat empty stomach; the green his neck, sinewy as a branch growing out of the slim trunk of his torso. He had kept the child's dangerous perception of things as all a part of one whole; a warm stove part of a warm hand; cold feet themselves stone; had not the expertise or technique to separate one image from another and was literal-minded.

Yet he was as adult as any master in his awareness of the mechanics of inspiration; knew precisely the spectrum of feelings that measured this fluency; knew when it would be better just to sleep or play with friends or bring in logs for the fire. None of these actions were done for themselves or for the sake of those who associated them with recovery and balance. They were done because his head was empty: devoid of a glow which was like a fire lit.

That morning the river had made him think of snakes. He was fifteen and he wanted to paint snakes. Not anatomised and precise, but as long, sinuous swims of colour on a background of sea.

But he had to go to school.

The school was a small affair in the centre of Villereau, manned by three teachers who were vital in their strictness but not in their teaching. Pierre felt their greyness enter his pores the moment he walked through the gates. And it was not a greyness in which one could relax. Oh no, there were constantly things to do: neatly move hand from left to right, stand up, sit down, file around. And if one was out of step even a fraction, everyone saw. Everyone saw if the sonnet did not scan, which it did not because Pierre had not the words to make it do so; or if the map was wobbly, which it was for he had no precision with shapes that had to be copied; or if the figures did not add up, which they usually did, for strangely Pierre liked the delineation of right and wrong. So one could not relax, could not be interested, and so just fidgeted. It was a school alive with fidgeting.

Sometimes an image would appear inside Pierre's head, three colours together, moving into a shape. He would watch carefully, and when they were just about to merge into a form tangible enough to sketch, the droning would intensify which meant it was directed at him, which meant he would have to do something, which meant the image would be lost. This imposition happened with infuriating regularity. And he could do little to stop it because if he did not get the right answer to questions that were no more than demands for regurgitation, the anger in the room swept his mind completely until even the grossest thought of what book to get out next became garbled. The fragility of a real idea stood no chance, and he would slump on his stool, set for irritation, the final target of which would be his mother as she coaxed him to food or rest.

Occasionally he managed to keep the two levels moving simultaneously, but that was even more perilous. For Monsieur Daguzan was starved, and when Pierre's answers resonated with the contentment of private fulfilment, the man would gobble them up and leave Pierre bland and dangling, while his own voice found a new spirit that made the class sit up. Which is a way to serve someone without them knowing, but is a sin when it happens as theft.

The river did not steal. It gave. Whenever he went there, he found a new vividness which made green more green than it was before, red more red and lines hard-edged statements in themselves rather than divisions between shapes. It was like a drug that resolved all problems; put back into perspective life's questions. He talked to it. And its answers were his own thoughts fleshed out and empowered, affirming again and again his ability, his specialness, of which he was not yet sure because circumstance had not yet proven it.

"Go on," its lap on the bank urged.

"Yes, go on, miss school. It's only one day. Bring your easel here. Paint outside in the air. If they find you out, I'll cover. I'll turn their heads the other way, so they don't see; secretly tie their bootlaces together so you can fly free. Trust me!"

It was delicious, this dabbling with the law; though he felt guilty when he saw Daguzan's slack face the next day. He had bloated himself on a pleasure and not shared it. But love is a knife that has to make cuts, even if they are in the third person in the triangle. Daguzan stood like a jealous child hugging himself, the more upset for not knowing what it was that had hurt him. His words were wisps of cotton that fell on his pupils as an irritation, while Pierre's silence was a rich drape that everyone wanted to touch. In the bleak playground he was invisible for being surrounded, while Daguzan drank coffee alone out of a silver tumbler.

By the time he was sixteen, Pierre's room had become a psychedelic storeroom: paintings everywhere, some large, some small; tiny replicas of single thoughts received in the quietness of the evening. He liked to sleep with them there, not narcissistically, but because they carried within them the river, and that made him sleep more peacefully. They made him feel complete and resolved; although the resolution was not apparent in his petulant movements around the house. To anyone who does not know about the grips of talent, it looked like simple selfishness.

One day, an uncle, whose wife was dying of tuberculosis, had come to see Pierre's mother. It was her birthday, and he brought presents, which made Marie feel sad because they were wrapped badly, and somehow the pending bereavement presented itself in the sugared almonds which a less preoccupied mind would have remembered she did not like.

The uncle had stood for a long time in front of Pierre's paintings trying to discern why they were good. The perspective was not right, the composition imbalanced, yet they had power. He spoke to Pierre about taking one or two of them to Paris to sell. Pierre was pleased.

"Maybe even fetch a little," Uncle Jean said clapping Pierre on his snaky back. Pierre felt strange when he said that, and the next morning the river had been unyielding and cold. There seemed to be conditions upon this gift.

As it happened, the paintings fetched nothing. But Pierre could not forget the promise. It hung in his mind like a lamp lighting a prized possession, picking out and making a commodity of its intricacies. He began to hanker after some recognition. For who, tempted, is not haunted by the prospect of exhibiting their wares, of saying, 'Look, this is mine. I did this!'

And it made him restless so that the river in his head had to leap and bump over the rocks which were the beginnings of desire. He tried to free himself, to become the empty vault he had been before, but instead the nervous searching came out in rejection of his family. They became the rocks he threw out with shrugs that stopped their hands from straightening cuff or collar. Their right over him had run out.

And he had spoilt his secret liaison with the river by turning it into a possession. And possession breeds possession so that he wanted the river more, to the point where every evening, without fail, he would make the long walk over the fields to the water; would rush over the letters and rows of figures that had been given identically to each one of the thirty school boys, some of whom were becoming young men now, growing hair on their chins, beginning to dream.

Pierre sat next to the butcher's son who was heavy. His boots were full on the ground, whereas Pierre's were thin and worn. He would curl his breeched legs under him, which made Daguzan shout sometimes, as though he were addressing in Pierre some hidden effeminate streak in himself, of which he was ashamed.

"Legs, Bonnefond, legs!" The shouting hurt Pierre's system, but he could not help his legs. They would twist under him without his realising and instantly Daguzan would be upon him again.

Anyway, he did the homework and would be off, telling Marie, who longed so deeply to believe it, a story about visiting Edouard or whoever of the thirty boys Pierre cared to lie about. She let him go and he would be there, watching the water. It saved her sewing to believe him, for when she let the lies affect her, her fingers slipped and made mistakes her unlined pockets could ill afford.

It was a small river, but it was curious how active the wildlife was around it. Birds which Pierre could not name and did not care about flew inches above it and, pulled to land, would hover, then shoot up and away. Some mornings, the noise of their singing was deafening and old men walking early to work would notice that the centre of the town was silent and cold.

The trees too seemed to bend to the river as if pulled. They were not heavy and should, with their slim, well-formed branches, have been upright and separate. Yet they were bunched together and dense. Pierre would shelter under them when cold, but mostly he liked to be out in the open, enjoying the freedom of the wide night. He would walk a little to rid himself of the smell of home and school, then find a spot to settle: a different spot each day, for the whole stretch of river should know him.

Seated, his back hunched and tense as though attentive to someone talking, he would scan the water with his green eyes, watch it, ripple by ripple, as it lapped against the bank. In the summer he would dabble his hands in it, lift out pieces of trailing weed and then drop them back again and splash his face with water. It was an innocent procedure, but had the sweetness of a caress.

His pictures were changing. His room had overflowed into the dining area downstairs and his mother was having to do an hour's more mending in order to buy his paint. Pierre did not register this as a problem for her, seeing only the perfect new bottles on his shelf. But Catherine did and it made her angry with her brother. She pulled his unfinished food from him in the mornings now. She was plump and jealous because Pierre's body was becoming beautiful; his face turning the heads of her friends, where his contemporaries were unmoved by hers. She felt he had snatched everything for himself and even though he did not concentrate at school, did well. He had bad writing, but she knew he was clever. Learned at home between bread making and washing, her writing was round like her body and could not be distinguished from Laura's, Beatrice's or Robert's. When they came for tea, they fingered Pierre's paintings and said he was brilliant - a childish exaggeration, but partly true.

One day, Monsieur Daguzan came to deliver Pierre's report. He had only to hand it over, but he stood awkwardly in the doorway, his cloak fastened tight around his pale body. He was drinking in the homeliness as he stood there; a power which available to him more often might have had him undo the hooks on his cloak, throw off his heaviness and relax. But alone, regimented, formal, his body was always cold - and never naked.

Usually one of the younger teachers delivered the reports to parents, but he had wanted to come himself because he felt confused by the fact that it ran the boy down when Daguzan knew the boy was aiming high. He wanted to say that to Marie, whom he also thought rather lovely because of her cakes and her roaring log fire which opened some knot in his spine - that, like his small collared shirt, was a symptom of his meanness. Daguzan had sensed an edginess in Pierre lately and he also wanted to warn his mother; not considering that she might already know.

Instead, the man found himself in front of the paintings. He could not have avoided them, spilling as they did into every room. They robbed him of what he was going to say, as the river made Pierre forget his sums. The fineness that was in the man came to the surface and he thought, 'Let the boy go mad, let him, but he must go on painting.'

The paintings he saw were green and blue mainly, but more red had slipped in lately. Red for some reason was more expensive than other paint. It cost several more seams, which strangely was how it appeared on the canvases: long, red lines contrasting with the roundness of the greens, or with the objects the boy painted: his mother, his uncle, the river itself, the pathway that led from the field down through the woods. 'Yet it is the colours that strike one,' thought Daguzan scratching his livery cheek.

The red had come in strongly one morning. Pierre had only a dried out bottle of red, but he had spent over half an hour digging a stick into it and with the little he managed to scrape out, had lined the trunk of a tree with streaks of blood.

Now he wanted yellow. Desperately, as others in his class wanted desperately the baggy trousers that were replacing the breeches in Villereau so that they dreamt of them and chivvied until the tailors were sold out. That badly, he wanted yellow. When he got it - a set of dress hooks' worth - he painted his best picture yet.

It was his mother's birthday again. Uncle was coming. Aunt Jeannie was dead now and Uncle Jean brought only flowers which he purchased from a stall on the way. Pierre guessed he would want to take the picture to sell. And he was right. He stood in front of the yellow images, flowers still in his arms, while Catherine was fetching Marie down.

It seemed a long time before he turned, but when he did, Pierre thought he was crying. It was cold out. Maybe it was that. Or the red. Maybe he did not like the red. Pierre was not sure, so he pretended he had seen no tears. He was shy, did not like emotions on the face, only in paint.

"I shall take your picture to Paris. This one will sell," said the man quietly.

When his uncle had left, Pierre slipped out, calling to Marie, in a voice too distant for recrimination, that he was going for a walk.

The river was cold again. He sensed it as soon as he was within fifty yards. His mind started to panic.

"What's the matter? What is it?" He talked to the river, but its cold persisted and no colours came.

Pierre sensed it was because Uncle Jean had taken his fire picture to sell, but did not sense that he was being protected against a false independence, a claim to fame to which he had no right. The hand that moved across the canvas was his own, but the mind that guided it was not.

No more colours or shapes came for three days. He did not pick up his paints at all. The brush, which seemed to carry in its slimness all the fullness and feeling of the river, became a stick in a pot of water. He still went to the river, but it was bleak because before it had been bliss.

Before, climbing over the stone stile, walking through the woods, down the steps, leaves wet and fragrant underfoot, had been so sweet, for it preluded intimacy, secrets, new ground, so that he was learning in a year what took Chagall a lifetime to learn. He knew he was being shown the private, quick way to mastery. But his mistake was in thinking that the mastery was his own and the results of it public.

Pierre had grown tall in this year filled with adult lessons, and he stood tall by the river, his hands digging at the lining of his pockets, a nail catching on a lumpy darn done by his mother who, having renounced expressing his affection, still did her duty to her son's body. There was a hard discomfort in his brain. His thoughts moved fast and superficially, and there was no glow when he walked into the house, but for that of the fire in the hearth.

For the first time he began to notice his mother's face, how tired it was; his sister's body, how fat it was, and he longed to be with them, to make a joke, to see them laugh. But they had moved too far from *him* now in an effort to survive his strangeness.

On the fourth evening after his uncle had left, Pierre went again to the river. It was different. The water moved to meet him. It was *his* river again. The relief was so intense he wanted to shout and run, but he let his breath and heart do that while he stood still, eyes shut, waiting. Nothing. The warmth was still there, but no colours formed to take back to his canvas.

Into the blankness, changing now into peace, slipped a new thought. That he should enter the river. It was cold outside his mind. The trees were frozen and the moon itself seemed to shine coldness into the water. The thought came again: 'Enter the water.'

'It will be all right,' he told himself.

It was frightening, but the thought was sweet. He felt the fear and the sweetness simultaneously. The sweetness was getting stronger. It came from inside him, yet it was not him, for he knew the danger of cold, dark water. It entered his legs. They walked slowly to the bank. Another thought came: 'Sit down.'

He sat.

'Put your head forward.'

He felt ridiculous sitting there like a child who cannot dive, tipping forwards into the water. He sat like that for some time, knowing in a detached and clear way that in a very few moments he would be a body amidst the dark underwater weeds. The sweetness kept pulling. His head bent between his knees, he became a ball, toppled and in his dark cloak became a part of the dark water.

It could not rise to meet him, break its banks to enter him, so *he must lose himself in it*. He must disappear in order to draw it into his body: water moving through his veins to his heart and brain, coursing through him like blood. For life with just mother, sister, school, was no life. It was a nauseous droning along a long, flat path. The river was hills, valleys, green, deep, velvet.

So there was no choice.

When they found him, his cloak was wrapped around his head. There was a smile underneath, but removing the material had jerked his mouth into a crooked line. His eyes were closed, though the spirit behind them was more open than it had ever been.

Lifted away from his body on a cradling expanse of light, on wings for his tired mind, he had been rocked, held and forgiven for his suicide by the fire-fly part of him that, once the instigator, then the quiet observer of his strangeness, was temporarily his protector.

And inside that brief embrace, he saw what can only be seen when one is unafraid: that he had been influenced; that his whole, short life had been empowered by a talent not his own. He was like a millionaire who crashes, yet is heady on his own poverty.

It had not been his fault that he had grabbed at riches. His life had simply been a bid to get back what he had once lost. For who with empty pockets will not work to fill them; who with a hole in a wall will not plaster it; who with a patch of bare earth in a garden will not plant flowers there; who, in a shop seeing soft velvet next to the gauze she has come in for, will not finger the velvet more readily, buy it and set it into a garment that becomes her identity?

And now the unfurled velvet he had clothed his life in folded over his body under the bright morning sky.

Villereau was horrified and Pierre's mother and sister became knitted together in a sorrow that they could not shake off until they went too.

The picture did sell. To a gentleman with a monocle in a salon in Paris; a man as distant from the trembling of an idea forming and a paint brush thrust into red water as a French peasant is from the sequinned boleros that were in fashion. But tortoise-shell eyes saw quality and fingered bank notes as Uncle Jean stood proudly.

Monsieur Daguzan was at home. He had not taught Pierre for a year now, but had continued to feel his presence as colour in the greyness of the school which he longed to leave but could not because there was nowhere to go for a man who caught four colds a year and had no drive. He sat at his old table by the fire and started looking again through the newspapers: he faintly recalled another incident at that river... Every day after school he searched. Placing his watch and chain in front of him, he would time himself for an hour and a half. It was the eleventh week and the eleventh time that he had started by thinking: 'Why didn't I tell his mother about his instability? Why didn't I warn her?' He saw himself again standing in the doorway, thanking, turning, the paper bundle of cake which she had given him sticking out of his pocket, his eyes too full of the pictures to say anything about the boy he had come to love. And now he was dead.

On the twelfth month, a Thursday, he found it. The article was yellowed but clear: "On 8 July 1690, Mademoiselle Valerie Jouvance was found drowned in La Riviere Sainte." Daguzan, his every fibre alert, read on. She had been a clever girl, the daughter of the headmaster of L'École de Laurence - and a gifted artist. Prior to her death her first painting, entitled 'La Flambe du Coeur', had sold in Paris.

Daguzan shivered. He put on his cloak and went out into the snow. The knowledge pounded in his head. He had found what he was looking for. He had found Pierre's passion. But he had found it as a passer-by might spot in a shop window a diamond that he can not afford, and so can never hold in his hand. It was a faint gleam behind glass rather than an intricate structure of ever-changing colours. Likewise, only the most obvious aspect of this coincidence could Daguzan see, though the tension in his head pointed to the more complicated link between the two young people.

Dirtying the last piece of clean snow on the sidewalk with his boot, Daguzan wished he could feel an ounce of that complexity for the middle-aged mademoiselle that delivered a jar of marmalade to his house each week with something more in mind as payment than 'thanks'; but even the marmalade he found rather bitter.

He walked for an hour in a disgruntled stride through the slush, slipping sometimes and cursing. It was himself not the weather he damned; his nervous teetering on the boundaries of a world he could never quite enter.

Finally he decided to turn back, as a half-hearted climber might turn back from a mountain when it starts to drizzle with the justification that it will turn into a blizzard. He began to feel better as he walked: up the hill past the trellised gate to Monsieur LaMarche's sloping garden, past the gap in the wall where the stone steps linked with the high road, past the statue of the unknown child on horseback set in gravel and behind railings. Yes, he was feeling better and better on this home ground that he trod. He knew its little ins and outs, down to the bump in the road by the potter's house of which he had heard that many a visitor had fallen foul.

And returning to Number 4, Rue de Chasse, the gleam of the knocker in the snow-brightened sun was a welcome. Daguzan had exhausted himself over this boy. It was better he should rest.

Pierre too had exhausted himself. He was like a blind person who, without the distraction of eyes, cannot rest in the superficial but must see the invisible story; must know by the ebb and flow of energy in a room where there is attraction and where love. The former had powered much of Pierre's life, and the fast succession of untruths this had led to passed in front of him, making him feel that it was he who was moving; though, in reality, he was being held still in an aura of light.

A touch of which fell as consolation upon Daguzan, who took tea from a tray in his small, dingy sitting room and looked, in his stillness, much like a dark-framed portrait of a Dutchman. It only needed the chequered floor, the heavy curtain behind him...

LIONEL

*Only a child embracing
the thick trunk
could tell his heart
was full of oaken knots.*

He was like a blind person who, without the distraction of eyes, cannot rest in the superficial but must see the invisible story...

He drew them with his laughter. He was fat and had not the wit of some of his friends, but his laughter was a magnet that pulled the whole room close to him. People hung on his words, their pupils gleaming like pinheads, and they forgot whatever petty horridness they had caught themselves in. In turn, they made him forget that he was missing a piece of himself. With their round approval in his head, he felt full, and he sat by the fire, spindly legs outstretched in front of his bulk, like a happy cat.

It was an uneasy time. The English countryside no longer seemed as free and quiet as it had been. The railway snaked across the landscape - an intruder - while in the fields it divided, small boys died of cold, their stomachs filled with raw turnip. When Lionel thought about this, it joined with his own brokenness and made a double sorrow. Laughter was a disguise, clothes pulled on fast to hide an ageing body.

As his guests swilled hot wine, he raised an arm in the air, pretending to be the new church steeple. Local folk had written fiery letters about this, projecting onto that steeple with its jazzy buttresses, all their resentment about the changing horizon. He knew how they felt, and with his other arm he played out the birds landing on it cawing, his loose mimicking lips pulled into a long 'O' so that his tongue fell back: rather like his son's had done the year before when he was hung for rape. And in Lionel's sympathy was a shadow of mockery for their noisiness over a situation so much less important than an unjust death.

It was this sharpness that made his humour work, for they were afraid of his sudden flip from banter to malice. When that angular, red face turned on them, they became cautious. But it was a good sport to duck the arrows and watch them hit someone else, and they began to think of him as a candidate for election after all. He, who had just been endearing, had become powerful; had the mystery that sometimes surrounds a person who has suffered tragedy. And they watched him with the fascination of an audience as he took the stage.

Between the lines, Lionel's eyes were blank and sad because, to this day, he could not fathom whether his son had been guilty. He had combed his childhood, his young manhood and brief adulthood, trying to find the weakness in his make-up; put his finger on what had happened. But even the deepest part of his mind, which could touch on anyone's concealed weakness, could find nothing in Charlie but innocence and vitality. He had been a religious boy, and although at one time his love for the Bible had worried Lionel, his doubts were always assuaged by Charlie's energetic presence. It defied his piety.

And at the end of each day as he lay awake, invariably later than Rosie, whose sleep had not been affected; while other things had, like the steadiness of her hand, her memory - 'Lionel, did we eat that pheasant or not? Lionel?' - he always came to the same point: that he did not know what lay behind this strange event, and that he therefore had not known his son. This particularly upset him because he thought they had been utterly connected, perhaps not in the ideal father and son relationship, but as two spirits, interdependent as day and night.

Lying, solid yet restless, Lionel remembered himself at fifteen: standing in a gang of boys on the Green to watch a cockfight; hearing his own voice in high-pitched mimicry of his mother's small talk. Had anyone else imitated her, he would have punched them. But seeing his friends' faces break into smiles and receiving the smack of dirty but congratulatory hands on his back (those same hands that now offered tidy handshakes at his parties) he had realised that he had found a way to be popular: he could make people laugh.

Then he thought of Charlie at the same age: gentle, earnest; volunteering to carry the sack of pheasants when they were out shooting; bringing home abandoned lambs, putting them in the corner of the stable and watching them strengthen as he and Thomas groomed the horses; wanting them to be all right as much as he wanted his political father to be successful, his hostess mother popular.

Lionel was filled with self-hatred at the stark contrast between them. He wished he were the self-contained one rather than the taker; the one who relied for his strength on the affection of friends.

He was unable to see that compulsion lay behind Charlie's giving as much as behind his own taking; that sacrifice as much as humour is a demand for an audience; that he and the boy were simply the embodiment of two extremes which would eventually meet and balance.

The glimmerings of clarity and yet distress at the direction of his thoughts - should he not be straightforwardly mourning? - made Lionel pad nightly into the hall like a fat ghost stalking to where the fire burnt low.

Once their maid had met him, having woken early herself; afraid she had missed the dawn and would be scolded by cook for not stoking the fire. She saw his large back bent over the grate and coughed politely. He jumped, distress reversing his reflexes so that it seemed he might fall into the fire. But he managed to steady himself and turned to her.

"What is it, Mary? What are you doing down here?"

"I woke up by mistake, Sir," she answered awkwardly, her legs, which looked as though they had been put on back to front, still shaking. "I thought it was time to stoke the fires. Why are *you* here, Sir?" Had the sun been up and she dressed in her starched collar and dress, and he not in his cotton gown, legs visible, she would not have dared to ask. But they were equals in the night.

"I couldn't sleep," he answered.

Mary's heart raced. Four years ago she had been Eppie's maid; herself a child then; and Eppie, dismissive, and unaware of a child's tendency to remember, had confided to the maid her fantasies. At first Mary had been shocked but then, bemused by Eppie's pretty face and fine clothes, had laughed and rather enjoyed knowing that Eppie's body desired and raced with hot little shivers during the night. She had even seen it once with her own eyes. When she heard about the rape, she was certain that Eppie must have lured Charlie down and that it could never have been his fault.

"Sir, that Miss Eppie was a naughty girl," Mary blurted out.

"She used to tell me all her secrets, and I'm right certain that she must have made him to do it, Sir. You must believe that, Sir." And blushing from her boldness, she bobbed and turned, mumbling, "Er, good night, Sir."

For a second, Lionel allowed the scene of the hanging, now a permanent image in his mind, to be bathed in light. But when Mary had gone, the light went with her, and it was just a hanging again. He spoke after her into the darkness, in a voice both unforgiving and distraught:

"But it's always the man's fault, Mary."

Broken sleep made Lionel a tired man; a man who had little control over his senses. He ate and drank heavily and his laughter was spiced with garlic and sausage and fear. During the past year, his jokes had become more absurd, more visual, absorbing the energy in his arms that might otherwise have hit the men who had decided about his son's life and who continued to make decisions too fast because their fields had to be sown and so they had not the time to think.

At the one or two annual hangings a year, the whole town would be present. The people that now sat in his drawing room, warming their hands on goblets of hot wine, only last July had watched, from either far or close, his son's feet dangle over the gallows and his head drop as now their heads dropped to retrieve spilled food or recover their laughing breath; breath, his son had not recovered.

Every movement Lionel made, either in the public ritual of his parties or in the private sustenance of his land, was threaded with the daytime image of young Charlie. As they stood to thank God for tender lamb, he remembered Charlie carving his first joint. As he sat to eat, taking the linen cloth from the brass ring to wipe his chin, he remembered Charlie in the brewery making his first ale, watching the jugs froth, and coming out one day with a white moustache, having tasted before time.

As he went on pouring, the thinking went: 'Maybe that was it, maybe it was drink that did it.' It had come up in the inquiry, but there was no evidence; nothing to suggest under what circumstances he had brought Eppie down to the ground in the trees behind the lodge that Thursday.

As the evening wore on, he would live Charlie's troubled birth - 'Lionel! That's it, I'm going. This'll kill me, Lionel! (He desperately pacing the hall below) Lionel!' Blood spattering, women rallying with hot water... Then, Charlie's tenth birthday party... Charlie's first piece of prose...

It was exactly the same sequence each time. He had seen that tenth birthday party over thirty times since last year, yet whenever the scene came to him, his laugh came too: like a great draught of medicine to stop him from breaking, and to shield him from the silent night when his mind was flighty and unsettled. He was like ground that has been broken by the uprooting of a huge tree. It was not just a son he had lost but a part of himself.

Lionel was a Christian. He had never considered that he might have lived before. Charlie had only been Charlie and he only Lionel. Yet the sense of loss; the sense that life without the boy would be a meaningless crawl up a very steep hill, challenged the singleness of the relationship. And because it was a challenge that only his soul not his brain could understand - for the soul lives many lives while the brain lives only one - he thought he was going mad.

"He is a marvellous man, isn't he?" Marcia Ellis said to her husband as they walked out of his gate into the darkness. "It is marvellous how he manages to cope in the face of it all."

"He looks very well indeed," agreed her husband. "In fact, he seems to be more jovial each time we see him."

Neither of them realised the fact that marked change, whatever its form, should be reason to be wary.

"She doesn't look very good though, does she?" Marcia remarked, a little of the malice, that had made her stand fifty yards from the hanging, rather than a hundred, appearing on her half-obscured face. The air was crisp and clean, but when they reached their home, they fell into bed, blunted by food and drink. They loved Lionel as the whole town did, but not enough to stay awake for him.

Lionel was standing in the hall as the rest of his guests took their leave. An uneasiness filled his head, and his thin legs shook a little as he bear-hugged, kissed faces turned a little to the right and bade his guests farewell.

What had been a shadow during the evening began to travel the nerves of his brain. Whether they were nerves to activate his arms to wash, his eyes to scan the accounts, his hands to lift his horses' feet into the air to relieve them of flints that could not be retrieved by his lazy groom (who was kept on because he had grown up with Charlie and had crumbled a little at his death and had maybe... maybe known a bit more than he had ever let on); whatever nerves they were for, they all juddered with this one new thought from his soul: that Charlie had done it on purpose; had wanted to be strung up there in front of the townsfolk and have his neck broken. He had planned it.

Lionel went out to the stable. The groom was sitting there almost under the horse's belly. Lionel watched him from the doorway. The boy should have been at home in the cottage let to his mother and her five other children. Why was he here? Why was Lionel himself here? It was late. But he was here and the boy was here and Lionel's laughter had left him, so he asked the boy outright.

The boy was nervous because it was the first time Lionel had spoken without clapping him on the back or gently punching him in the ribs; the first time he had heard the man's voice hard, straight and quiet. It was the voice that connected with his grieving legs not his belly.

"What do you know about my son, Thomas?"

Thomas' mouth jiggered and a hand went to his red furry ear. The scene between him and Charlie had happened right on the spot where he and Lionel were now standing.

"Yer lad were no more guilty than oy am, though 'ee did it royt enough." Thomas had no words for the rest of the story. He just knew that Charlie had a good reason. Charlie had explained it to him, after all. He had told him that the only way to get Lionel into power was to show the town he was brave in the face of tragedy. Charlie had hardly understood his own intentions and he had chosen Thomas as confidant because he knew that he would not understand them at all. It was just the feeling of release he needed that comes from the listener revering you, regardless. Now, Thomas was a child throwing bits of a jigsaw at a grown up. Angry, upset, saying, 'You do it.'

Lionel picked them up, and with the insight of the desperate rather than the skilled, he pieced them together, bitterly remembering that a week ago he had received a letter informing him of his nomination. Charlie's plan was working.

Thomas was calm now that he had made an attempt at owning up; calmer than he had been for a year. And Lionel stood still on his spindly legs. He knew Thomas was throwing him diamonds but it was his habit as master to be stern.

"Thomas, what you've said is rubbish. Charlie was a noble lad but he was no Jesus Christ. Come on. Tell me the truth."

"Tis the truth, Sir," Thomas repeated.

"Thomas."

"Yez, Sir."

Lionel looked into his face which was barely distinct from the rest of his body, and tried to read it, but the light was too dim. Thomas put his hand on the horse's flank and said nothing.

"Thomas."

Still nothing.

"Come on, Thomas."

Thomas took his hand off the flank as though help from the animal he had spent most of his life with and had talked to in rhythm with the to and fro of his grooming brush - 'La-dy, La-dy, I love Dai-sy, Dai-sy. She-do, she-do, she-do not-love-me not-love-me, do-she, do-she' - was now yielding nothing. He tried his pockets instead.

"Said'ee owed ye summat," the boy blurted out. (Lionel's night-time self stirred and listened.) "Ee kep' sayin', 'oy owes im a lot.'"

I says: "Wot, for bein' a good pa, loyk?"

"Ee says: "No, summat more an' that. 'Ee's important and he needs an important deed." Sometimes 'ee would look loyk 'ee were goin' to cry when 'ee said that. It was like a great spurt of feelin' in 'im. An' that's all oy know, Sir. An' oym royt sorry, but now I'm goin' 'ome."

What Thomas was trying to explain was a phenomenon hazy to even the most articulate: of why people do what they do. For what logic was there in a rape to secure a father's social position? What force so strong could lead a man to death for a cause so ephemeral as politics? Men on Tibetan hillsides may better understand this. Men who exist silently in the space between life and death, who put aside the distractions of the body may understand how much bigger and deeper is motivation than is apparent. Thomas was stumbling upon it as Lionel had in the night and both were frightened by it.

Lionel stood in the stable which echoed the silence of the Tibetan hillside. The drinking and conversation of the evening seemed distant. Lady peed into the straw and cut the silence. Lionel laughed, but it was weak, sinister laughter; like a former friend, repulsed by vulnerability, leaving for the winning side.

He was extraordinarily lonely. If he had had to stand up the next day and make a speech about housing the poor, he could not have done it. He might have crumbled in the middle, lost his way, forgotten the figures. The smart quipping of the Town Hall seemed a world away.

And though he had seen the illusion of success, his disillusionment and tiredness became anger; a self-condemning anger that he could not be a Lambert; also that people like Lambert always win. Lambert, his rival in the elections, was straight-backed and precise. He was smooth and unbroken, all the sinews of his body compact and aligned. Lionel's breeches rucked up and he smelt of fear. They loved him, but they would never follow him. Not with the strain this new discovery would put on his laughter; that fragile gift which, until now, had seen him through.

There were four more parties that year. They were everybody's landmarks as they struggled through the colder weather. For the first of them at least, Lionel coaxed his humour back with drink and it served him more or less. Enough to have Tom Smith guffaw in a corner, "Thank the Lord for Lionel." But not to silence the whole room as once it had.

And when a wiry little man (a Lambertite) rejoined, "Quiet though, innee?" Lambert himself heard the exchange and multiplied it until a bed had been made, relations rallied, herbal potions dreamed up for the man they had planned to have a breakdown. They chewed on his weaknesses as noisily as they did on the tough pheasant that Mary brought on a platter, guilty that she had got it out of the oven late because she had had a bad day. 'Most days are bad now,' she thought.

The last of the parties was Lambert's own. It was a celebration. He had won his place in parliament and he wished to thank, graciously, those who had made it happen. His long fingers clasped the stem of a goblet. He had twisted his voters around him with the same ease, not needing to sit with his legs crossed tightly, protectively, hoping. He knew he would win. His sentences ended in full stops not question marks. He did not apologise though he was sometimes wrong (if judged by the Tibetan monk, very wrong indeed) or forget to smooth his hair down. His routine had him sit up in bed at five, his cheeks round and rested, as though the soul in him had tucked itself into his head for the night and stayed there; while Lionel's tried to get out, to be free - residence in his acid body being uneasy.

Charlie's plan had veered off. He had not watched carefully enough; had been moved only by his own need to repay the man and by his recollections of Lionel's strength. He had remembered him as his 'father' in the woods, screwing his eye to the barrel and shooting, then standing up slowly and casually before sending the boy with a signal to fetch the hot body of the bird from the grass; remembered the time Lionel had stood up from the audience in the Town Hall and spoken concisely and venomously about enclosures; remembered his gentle instructions given the night before the boy's first riding lesson; and with a very distant part of himself, remembered the man's bravery as soldiers pushed him viciously up the hill to his death; remembered all those strengths and built of them a picture that painted over the cracks in the old soul of the man.

But the boy's poignant sacrifice had not been wasted, for it robbed his father of laughter, the last talent he had, and left him empty. Now, light and strange, without the stabilising presence of other people's affection, he could be carried easily to something more enduring than political success. He was a spiritual man, and it was to his spirit that life attended. Spirit and public recognition had been indistinguishable to Charlie at twenty - if one wins, one is good - yet the integrity in the boy's intention had carried the plan regardlessly in the right direction. And as for the final settling of business between them, there would be another time, another place...

When Lionel lay down to die on a summer morning, when the same group of elms that had made the box Charlie had kicked at his hanging were swaying like drunken men, he was more frightened than at any other approaching death of his existence because he was dying without anything to look forward to. His despair blanked out the sense, usually so sweet, of a protective cluster of people to receive him; a mother, a father, a sweetheart. This death was a grey nothingness; a slipping out of one flesh and into another, and he resisted it.

Which was why Rosie, crying into the night, became a little more frail than ordinary mourning called for; as though her dear husband were seeking asylum in her head. She felt herself struggling to fend off an intruder.

For dead, outside warm flesh, Lionel was no more her husband than any soul.

She did not know what was happening, but five months later, at two in the morning, half sleeping words came forcefully from her: "Go! Go!" And he left her.

Four years later, she married Lambert.

LISA

Tethered to memory,
the yew waits
in the graveyard,
her sinewy arms clutching
at past lovers.

This death was a grey nothingness; a slipping out of one flesh and into another, and he resisted it...

Lisa sat on the veranda in the dusty afternoon wishing with all the might of her small body that she could walk over to the middle of the piazza and tell the man who was holding his child too hard by the hand to be more decent. But she could barely move her hands let alone her legs. All she could use were her thoughts, and they seemed hardly likely to penetrate the sandy head of the man she now recognised to be Nico, as he dragged the child to the statue where he would meet his wife.

So instead, she turned her head away and watched the birds digesting their stomach's worth snatched from the fat hands of chattering women who came daily with old bread and scraps of news to exchange. She watched how their full bodies balanced on stick legs not unlike her own, but then how those legs would merge into some prepared corridor in their feathers and the round balls would fly up and away to the sea. She watched birds as much as she did people. They offered more hope in their upward movement than did the human figures always lunging forward as though they could not see.

Lisa's own sight had been impaired as a child. She knew about living in the dark confines of limbs; relying on sensations of hard or soft; which was why she could see so clearly how people did not look. In fact, she had systematically been without almost every faculty at one stage or another. Her illness was thorough, creeping around her body in a mobile knot of energy. But it had no solidity and so no name. At present it was seated in the small of her back, sometimes splaying outwards in a flame of tension making the tips of her stiff fingers jerk, but mostly resting as white heat in the base of her spine.

Her hair was surprisingly healthy. It was fire's gentle form: soft and golden. And the calm contrast it offered to the havoc pain had wrought on her face made people comment on it, which they might not had it been the pride of a debutante.

Only once had Lisa herself hoped she might get better and then only for a moment. A visitor had come to the house. The round warmth of the woman had made Lisa easy and relaxed. She watched her hands as they picked up a vase from the drawing room table; how they held it so softly. And she felt it was she they were holding and all the old hurt and tension lifted away from her. In that fleeting moment she had glimpsed from the woman's hands the potential niceness of life; of how it might be to walk in a wood or wear new clothes. But then the butler had come to the door. He was a tall, straight-backed man. He only came to ask if she wanted tea, but he cut the atmosphere with his knife-body and the warm current that had been moving into Lisa was deflected.

They knew nothing of what they were doing. The woman did not know to what extent her sympathy was a healing power, nor the butler the degree to which his precision was harshness. They were simply the puppets of the girl's unconscious; there to act out what had started as a doubt and had escalated into a battle. And a battle will always find actors to represent it, often virtual strangers. The woman represented a reprieve from the babyhood decision Lisa had made to withdraw; the butler the toughness of a decision upheld.

Lisa's doctor, on the other hand, was quite uninvolved. Though his cold, dry hands regularly prodded her body, they touched her less than the soft swish of this woman's skirt on the rug. He was just a clever lame duck scratching away at little bits of clue. When he and his colleagues, sitting in a high-ceilinged study, arrived at Lisa on their list, a tiredness came over them and they wondered if it was time to open the wine which was standing on the sideboard. And when an elderly doctor took the plunge (knowing it was early yet), the others jumped in after him as if they had not had a drink for ages, though the meeting had begun with sherry. After their drink, they more easily put aside Lisa's notes and took out those of a man with gout. And it was a piece of cake, because gout is a matter that can be dealt with, while Lisa had made herself a cloud: intangible let alone curable.

Eventually, by formal letter, headed in italics, they broke the news to Signor and Signora Rosetti that there was nothing they could do.

Lisa was relieved. She was sick of hands scanning her chest and those quiet questions which missed by miles the target of her sickness and only hit her mother who longed for something with a name to ease her inflamed sleep. But the letter finally broke the woman's thread of hope and it dangled free in a resigned vagueness. The sickness had pushed her away; it, not she, was controlling Lisa. The little parcels she brought from overseas were the same; the reporting of daily news about new cushions, rolls of silks, the pending visit of her uncle from the south, went on as before. But the words held only their own meaning, where before they were filled with hidden messages of affection and concern.

So now Lisa was beginning to be left alone, to live with the illness which, as a baby, lying in a wooden bed at night, while her parents were at the opera, Lisa had instinctively called to herself so that one day she could be free to avoid the game of submission and role-playing that was implicit in growing up. For she was tired of trying to please, tired of being influenced, tired of attachments and estrangements. And besides, she needed quietness. And those inquiring minds were like people passing by an artist who wants to complete his painting unobserved.

Her parents had wondered about leaving her that September night, the night of her first birthday. But Signor Rosco had offered them tickets - it was Monteverdi - and at one year old she would hardly mind. Besides, they had fed her with coloured milk and kisses earlier in the day, laughing into her face, Mario's breath folding over her in alcohol waves. He was so thrilled with her smile, how it kept breaking again and again on to her lily face. She had paler skin than they. She was theirs but might not have been.

They had hugged her good-bye, her father lifting her high into the air and her mother caressing her downy skull, and they had giggled as they tripped down the stairs leaving instructions with Mona to check on her periodically. They were not to blame. Their farewell was affectionate and they had left her in safe hands. But a travelled soul is fragile: tending to register an unsmiling face as hatred, a momentary departure as abandonment.

Lisa connected Mario and Laura's innocent evening of celebration with a recognised pattern of abandonment. Her baby mouth opened to scream for the parents she hardly knew, closing and opening like a fish moving through deep water. No sound came. If it had, the seed of a disease that was planting itself in her body would have blown away like dust. For it is those who keep quiet who get ill, not those who scream.

She drew the illness into the emptiness inside her. It was a blessing she chose as clearly as she had chosen people, talents, affections, to inhabit her in previous births. Illness would give her room to conquer the fear that met her at every turn, whether the way looked initially clear or not; the fear that she was only half a person; that she would always need someone else to fulfil her; that she would go on and on accepting this rape of her spirit.

The balance of births is perfect. For every demanding role, there is a quiet one. King becomes subject, warrior becomes homemaker. But for some, intensity comes in a run until the person puts up their hands and says, "No more". Then across the ether, a wheelchair slides beneath them in an invitation to rest, and those who owe their apologies, their thanks or good wishes, come instinctively knowing that they are a part of the illness.

That night Lisa's hands had gone up. In the gap - whilst Lisa was dozing and Mario and Laura were beginning to lean forward, living out their own romance as they watched the final scene of The Marriage of Poppeia - the germ settled, peaceful and untroubling, preparing to explode into her limbs.

Mona had been woken by horses' feet after midnight and had pelted, skirts lifted, around the balcony to check her charge was safe. As expected, Lisa was asleep. Before Mario and Laura burst into the hall beneath her, Mona had brushed her hair, laced up her bodice and was there to meet them, her red head of curls hanging over the balcony, like a flag unfurled in the breeze, in greeting.

Her welcome was appropriate. They were happy, had drunk coffee with frothing cream on the way home and had enjoyed the mutual but delicious threat to their affection provided by the pretty people in the coffee house. Having kissed gently in the back of the carriage, they had tiptoed hand in hand up to Lisa's bedroom. They had stood there watching her, their perfect baby, seeing each other in her, and then quietly, their frivolity somewhat chastened, had left for their own room.

Three years later Lisa's legs went numb.

"Mama, Mama!" she had called, crumpled half way down the stairs.

"Mama, Mama!" It was a loud call from her depths and it frightened Laura desperately, made her scoop the child into her arms and rush her into the large drawing room.

She laid her child carefully on one of the empty chairs and started to feel her for broken bones. Lisa kept screaming and screaming. She had called to her out of shock, but now the power of her screaming catapulted the woman away from her to get help. She met Mona outside the morning room and ordered her to fetch the doctor.

"Quickly, or my baby will die... Where is Mario? Where is he?" She returned to the drawing room and waited, motionless as the china figurines on the mantelpiece.

Mona raced through the city streets and frantically banged on the doctor's door. The doctor had been sitting peacefully with a book and a glass of red wine, but he collected his bag and anxiously hurried with Mona back to the house. When they arrived, Laura was being sick in a rose-painted bowl while Lisa was under the charge of an involuntarily pregnant young maid, for whom this was a nasty prelude to motherhood.

And so it was that, even in the early stages, the illness touched everyone's life; like a liquidator come to wind up a business, and seeing extra accounts needing to be balanced, does those too.

And it persuaded the family to move away from Rome to a smaller town where the air did not chill one's bones; where Lisa could sit and watch its entire population amble from one side of the piazza to the other. This became her sole occupation.

Even in winter she insisted on remaining outside. Just in case *he* passed. *He* was the man with whom, out of all the hundreds, thousands of humans her soul had loved, there was business to settle. A virtual stranger now, he was the thorn in her flesh; though she did not know it. She did not know any more than the frazzled Laura knew why she insisted on being outside on the veranda, or why the doctor allowed it. Underneath her blonde mildness was a power which said, 'I want to be here and I shall be.' The Cardinal might pass. He might long for a breath of crisp air or to be free from the business that stressed him. He might - except that laudanum, kept in a small gold box intended for a relic, was more often his balm than exercise. He was impatient and neither the relaxation of a walk nor the slow power of prayer entered his nerve ends as quickly.

Lisa's conscious mind regarded the Cardinal, as dignified and intelligent, complete and aloof. Every Sunday when she turned her face to receive wine, he either coolly disregarded her or looked at her pitifully. Yet this did not deter her. Her days became significant only for the hours she spent under the white Italian sky watching out for him or in the frescoed church as he sang through the service. And the days became months and the months dusty years.

It was not until she was twenty that the right moment came. It was a bright September morning. She was sitting on the veranda sewing. Hearing voices, she looked up and saw him walking into the piazza amidst a group of cardinals and priests. They were in Napoli for a concordance. Cardinal Angelo stood in their midst like a hub. Though he had been outposted from Rome many years ago, no one had been quite sure why. He had all the qualifications to be useful in the Vatican.

She saw their deference to him, the way their long, thin bodies revolved around him like spokes, and because he was still for a moment, looking at the sky, they stopped too. She fell to thinking about her own inadequacy; how she was always on the edge of conversations because her body could not reinforce her words so they flew like the birds over the priests' heads. She thought, 'I am not like him. I am weak.'

Suddenly one of the spokes fell away. Crossing her thoughts at full speed, a black slant moved to the north of the piazza. Lisa had never seen a priest running before. She leant forward. What was going on? Her heart thumped against her bird-frail ribs.

He disappeared into a slit in the wall. People gathered from nowhere. There was running and commotion and noise. What had happened? She couldn't see. The priest returned clanking a wheelchair across the cobbles to the huddle of red and black. Lisa peered through her thick-rimmed spectacles. It was him: the hub; tiny, bundled over, his head on his knees. What was going on? She panicked as her mother had done, when Lisa had screamed from the stairs as a child.

They lifted the man into the chair, long white fingers joining to form a trellised seat for his half-conscious form. It was horrible, like seeing an oak lurch and fall or a General say sorry.

He was wheeled around and for an instant the yellow of Lisa's hair caught his eye. Either that, or maybe the sunlight made her seem to his blurred vision very bright. His eyes rested on her as if in doing so they could strengthen and steady themselves. Then he was wheeled away. So was Lisa, stunned by the force of his gaze.

He was a man, she a woman; he near the top of the tree, she at its unseen roots. But as bodies, they were for that moment equals.

They lay Cardinal Angelo on his bed. It had been a heart attack. He was to rest for a week. No services, no consultations, nothing.

"Just rest, Father, or it'll be the end of you, and that would be no good, would it?" Which it wouldn't, for his mission was not over. He had climbed the tree of his career carefully, placed one foot after the other with a precision the Vatican recognised - yes, certainly a man to be seriously considered - and yet each time his head was breaking through to the bare sky, his foot had slipped, and slimline officials struck him off. Once he had been spotted eyeing a woman; another time a rumour of ill-temper. And the combination of the world's ruthlessness and the knowledge of his own imperfection had brought him down into the cradling green leaves of mediocrity. For there was a darkness inside, a capacity to hurt, to disregard, ignore the leper's call and run. Lesser men would have made themselves insensitive, but he was the roots as well as the climber of the tree so he experienced everything.

And this attack (an inappropriate name for what he had brought upon himself) was his stopping midway. Physically ready to die and yet psychically more alert than he had ever been, he was a man moving with his feet tied. Until he could be forgiven, he would be unable to gather up the twigs and leaves of his religion and fashion them back into a solid branch which would not break under the weight of debate. For this was his future task.

Lisa had been put to bed. And the past, that a glance from the Cardinal had awakened, stretched itself in front of her in a dream:

They were standing on white sand outside a palace. Her crayoned eyes gazed into his. Then her arm, heavy with bangles, pointed to the red sky. It was evening and they were breathing in the sandalwood air. Silk wrapped soft and alive around their golden bodies. She put her cheek in the perfect arc between his head and shoulder. Music came to them from the huge veranda: timbrels and tambourines and women's song; an unbroken line of unnotated sound. As the sun disappeared, they remained silhouetted; a pale blue outline of their double form. They turned to each other, eyelashes touching, and rocked on the pinkened sand. Above them, a man stood. He watched their embrace with concern. He called to them. They did not hear. Again he tried, this time with a sharpness. The young Egyptian looked up. He knew that tone so well; knew it was time to go, time to leave this woman. He was ambitious. He had no choice. War and the daughter of Faranah (whom he loved so much less) were his duty. He pulled away, leaving the young girl's head unsupported. Then standing, he drew his energy back into himself like a man packing possessions before departing. He touched her face, made fire in her body with his fingertips, and walked away, up the wide stairs to the verandah where the man stood and disappeared through the wide doors.

It was Lisa he had left. Cold, nervous, with a pain too strong to be contained by stillness and silence. She tossed.

A new scene: zipping past her, horses ridden by men with feathered helmets. The cold of steel against her body, feathers in her mouth. Where is he? She scratched at the smooth flanks of the beasts and the solid bodies of the men. Where is he? Where is he? A group of eight galloping fast. She called. Her voice stuck, but her thought reached him. The horses slowed. There. He was bending down. To lift her? No, to adjust his stirrup. But resuming his upright position he saw her again with a new, solid, cold face; the chin she had cupped as a dark, unopened flower now set by a leather strap. Again she called. Dust blew in her eyes. He had gone.

She half woke, and in the clarity that often comes in first consciousness, she knew that abandonment was a state profoundly familiar to her. But the weight of that knowledge was too much and she withdrew back into sleep.

Mentally alongside her the Cardinal also dreamt, and though the images stirring in him were different, they told a parallel story: a beach. A ship. Lots of noise; shouting, gulls, joy. And a presentiment that everyone was leaving. But she was still standing on the sand. The ship that had come to fetch her was leaving without her. He was in front of her, fixed in a gaze that even the turning tide swirling around his feet had no power to break. A message was conveyed: an apology, in a language deeper than thought. Their eyes kissed. Then, swish from behind her, the drag of a boat on the sand. She turned, a hand helped her and she was rowed out to the waiting ship. He felt himself disappearing into a forest. He was calm.

One function of dreams is to reveal an exaggerated form of the truth: the hidden nastiness behind the proffer of help; the gross desire behind the casually bared leg. Another is resolution: to bring to a head a scene which daytime circumstances have reduced to a stereotyped exchange. The highest function of dreams is to reveal aspirations which lie way beyond the capacity of the present to express. The power in the last two lies in the fact that at some point they will manifest in action.

Lisa had all three kinds of dream. So did Cardinal Angelo, but more often the first. This disturbed him particularly when he woke from them to a Sunday morning. It was not fashionable (as it sometimes pretends to be now) for clergy to articulate their vulnerability, so donning his vestments seemed a dressing of his naughty soul, and it made him acutely uncomfortable.

The dream he just woke from - to the relief of not having to get up - was of the second kind. He felt a peace inside and told the nurse he was much better "thank you, and may I have something to eat?" She looked at him dubiously and said she would check with the doctor. He became tetchy, as is normal when spirit has been separated from body and tries to refamiliarise itself with matter too fast.

"I know if it's all right to eat, Nurse. It's my tummy." The nurse hesitated at the use of this puerile word. "Yes, mine!" he affirmed, denting it with his index finger. "And it's empty!" The nurse's broad foot curled in her shoe. His petulance irritated her and she unfairly compared him (being a man of God) to Jesus' benevolence with the loaves and fishes.

Lisa woke up and played solitaire. Her fingers enjoyed the cool roundness of the marbles and the neatness with which they rolled into the little mahogany dips. Her mother, walking stalwartly to the window, knocked her table. The coloured balls jumped out of their holes and clanked together, two or three rolling onto the floor. She felt strange. She had forgotten her dreams, though they continued to cling to her as an inexplicable sadness of which spoilt solitaire was a symptom. They were a job unfinished: too ephemeral to be a real settling between two souls. Lisa yearned for an unknown pleasure to which her dreaming self gave shape: touching this man, sliding her small white hands up his arms to his shoulders and pulling him close. And the need filled the air in the household with a purer power than an adolescent fantasy could have created; so powerfully, that Mario kept saying a storm was brewing and Laura could not sleep.

Cardinal Angelo, a determined man, was next Sunday administering wine at mass. He was moving slowly, concentrating as he lifted the cup so as not to make a mistake. The heart attack had shocked him into an anxious carefulness, though it made him appreciate what he had not noticed before: the domed ceiling, the chipped gold angel, and the grapes and curled sculptures that hung from the pulpit. It was giving him immense pleasure to experience his body again; like the pleasure of returning from a holiday, opening letters, smelling the rooms, opening the windows. He was in that lovely initial few days of return.

Most people consider the world unfair; that there is not much structure in the comings and goings of suffering. Crisis occurs and one responds; it eases and one relaxes. But that in itself is a pattern. There are always moments of relief, resting and preparing times. The agony of childbirth comes in waves, thunder in single claps, illness in stages. And not knowing what loveliness or peace may prelude, one drinks it greedily for its immediate taste.

The sacredness Cardinal Angelo was experiencing that sunny morning was just such a preparing time, for which his intelligent mind could offer no explanation. Indeed, everyone seemed to be in a state that charged their ordinary activities with intensity.

The first row of communicants resumed their seats, the ladies at pains to conceal rustle of dress and clack of boots. He looked up, took in the wide sweep of cool cathedral and breathed deeply. Then he saw Lisa's wheelchair approaching, pushed by Signor Rosetti. It disturbed his feeling of renewal; returned him to the moment of his collapse. Without knowing why, he wanted to avoid handing her the cup. But monarch, priest, politician are forbidden the luxury of choice; cannot refuse the hand in front of them. And so it was to Cardinal Angelo that Lisa came for her wine. He knew he was going to make a blunder; knew as one knows before a speech that one's nerves have gone too far beyond the healthy apprehension that preludes success. He had moved into shakiness. Why? He tried to pull himself together as he blessed the third communicant. Lisa was at the back of the queue, but a fear had come upon him over which he had no control.

She arrived in front of him. He had to serve her. He could see, then smell, the shine of her corn hair. Her face was near his chest which was tight with a memory he could not put into thought.

The cup slipped. Lisa's hands darted to catch it. So did his. She caught the stem, he the bowl, and their dithery fingers met.

"So sorry," he whispered.

"It's all right," she returned, embarrassed. But his whisper was a shout in her mind, and her answer a call to his spirit. It fell over him, softening the hard lines of his being. Ridiculously, his eyes watered. He wanted someone to hold his head, cup his chin, steady him, convince him it was all right, like a child who has behaved badly and is terrified of the consequences. His overriding awareness was that he had sinned; had lived his life in the shadow of a mountain he had refused to face.

He looked at the girl's face and saw only paleness and the lifelessness that comes of never being admired. Yet she seemed to assume the form and shape of his own being. He was looking at himself. This person robbed of life was what he had become, though he had been able to present to the world (as men can) an image of success.

A tenderness filled him. He wished he did not have to hold the cup, for it represented not absolution, but his job, his manliness, and it blocked from his sight this strange young girl for whom he had only ever had compassion.

Lisa was wheeled back down the aisle. A prayer was said, a hymn sung. A dusty beam of light shone through the coloured window. Along it travelled Cardinal Angelo's thought as he scanned the congregation. He wanted to keep in his vision this girl who had made his spirit leap, in case he should forget what her gentleness had allowed him to recognise.

He need not have worried. A storm does not pass with a single moment of lit-up sky. The room becomes light several times until sleep is renounced completely.

Lisa and Cardinal Angelo were in a realm of extremity. She extraordinary because her life was so bald; he, because he had just nearly died; and both, because their past and future were perilous but wonderful landscapes. In this realm, the storm cannot break quietly.

For the first time since childhood, the thought of wanting to walk possessed Lisa like a gust of wind roaring through a room. The wheelchair had been her home and protection for fourteen years. She was ready to leave it. As Signor Rosetti drew it beside him in the aisle, Lisa made a sound like a dog yelping. She had the braveness of the desperate. She eased herself up, hands gripping the sides of the chair and stretched her legs slowly so that she was standing on the foot rest, her form taller than everyone around her. The last verse of the hymn came to a close. Everyone turned. How ghastly! 'Why now,' her father thought, 'in front of everyone, when we have spent so many hours in our own home trying to help her?'

But she had not been ready. And besides, she was an actress at heart, and moments of change require an audience.

Lisa did not walk. Her raised form was enough to disturb the soft circles of sound that filled the air. Up she stood, like a bird poised to fly, and then plopped down again into the chair.

Later, her mother, who had been nauseous throughout the service, chided her severely, though she did conclude by saying how thrilled she was, of course, that the girl seemed to have a new will to live.

"I shall send you to Rome to stay with your aunt. There isn't much going on here to excite you. You can go to the opera and entertain yourself with your cousin," was how the conversation ended.

Which she did. And though her legs, adjusted to sitting, stayed weak, her mind opened to the colours and sounds of the Opera House. The actors moved for her.

A year later, chastened by illness and realisation, Cardinal Angelo received an invitation from the Vatican Secretary. He felt empty as he placed the letter in the drawer of his teak desk. Once he would have rejoiced, but now: 'If that is what you wish, Lord, so be it.'

And in that emptiness which ambition had previously filled, there was room for people's sorrow. He could listen, so he became the Vatican's chief advisor.

Lisa never saw him again.

LILY

The aspen is a querist
her mind trembles in the wind
like an arrow shattering.

She never saw him again...

"It doesn't matter," she said turning away. She meant it did and he knew it, but chose to leave it. They would come to it anyway. For the moment he wanted just to walk and pretend everything was all right, like a child turning over again to sleep though a voice is calling up the stairs.
"You go tomorrow, Simon."
"Yes."
"How is it?"
"I feel like a fish flapping on a gunwale," he said looking at a rowing boat bobbing a little way out from the beach. "Going back means you're half dead already."
She wished he would talk about himself directly and not in images. He wrapped everything up in a way her mind envied yet scorned, for it was a form of cowardice. She wanted him to stop walking, look at her and say, "Lily, I feel awful." Then she could comfort him. But there was no way in. Not even his appearance opened a door; no shadow, no nervousness; just a pushing back of his centrally parted hair. She was the flapping fish, not he.
Lamely she tried a question.
"Was it really bad last time, Simon?"
"Yes, but it doesn't matter."
He was using her words, inferring, 'Get out, I can't talk about it.'
He had been home for six weeks. Six long weeks. In a way, he wished to be gone. It was too hard this communicating business; this being ushered with kid gloves to recovery. Better to be at war, swearing, obscene, desperate, until it was over; better to just dream of leave, than to have it.
He had visualised every moment of this time in Aldeburgh during the lonely alertness of nights on watch. This seaside place was more

of a home to him than London. Westminster, where he had been brought up, his father a schoolmaster, had been too ravaged by the war to be remembered as a place of refuge. No, he had thought about walking right here, on the shelving shingle, under an evening sky. Then he had thought about the oddest luxuries like ironed underwear and putting up an umbrella. And there had been some crazy dreams, like the one of dancing with Lily along the pier: she dressed in turquoise, with a nipped in waist and a huge hat; he giving her flowers and she throwing them into the sea one by one so that they floated on the grey calmness and she laughing and thanking him; then his mother (not hers) chasing after them as if for her life, shouting, "Tea's ready. Tea's ready. It's ready. Simon! Lily! Come on now!" Then running back ahead of them as though to avoid danger and her shoe getting caught in one of the slats of the pier; they catching her up to help and Lily having uncontrollable giggles and Simon kissing her face flushed by the wind. Then the three of them - the slim heel of his mother's shoe still stuck in the pier and the flowers still on the water - going home together and eating huge slabs of chocolate cake.

His waking mind knew that they were all too tense and careful for any of that: Lily's face too closed, his mother's body too elegant to slip, and he too self-conscious for that easy harmony. His waking mind knew everything he wished to forget; so that, fingering Lily's letters, a fear had slipped in alongside the expulsion of the dream: that he did not know how to love. He looked at the other men; men he would never have chosen in civilian life but who were now his closest friends, for they had seen him terrified and weak. He thought, 'I bet you know how to love; bet you could get married and be happy for the rest of your life. I doubt if I could, even if it were someone other than Lily. There must be something wrong with me.'

It was the casual transfer of attraction, of which they were capable and he was not, that made him feel different from the other men. It cost them nothing to leer at Lily's photo, a dog-eared shot of her outside the Victoria and Albert Museum, because they would never have contemplated infidelity. They had their girls or their wives and they would stick to them. Their whistles meant nothing. But Simon knew that he was absolutely capable of deception; knew he would lie if he had to slip out of anything that tried too hard to hold him. One came to know those things about oneself at war. Even the little communal scenes, brave and grey in the dugout, spoke to one about the nastiness one was capable of. For war is as much about self-knowledge as it is about fighting; lived, as it is, as much in peace as in active aggression. Selfishness glared for everyone to see as did courage or gentleness. When one of them stole the sugared almonds sent by Simon's mother, a flare of anger filled the dugout, because they knew that if a chap could steal almonds he could just as easily kill one of them tomorrow.

In other ways, the dugout actually sustained the young man's deceptions. When it rang with wolf whistles and imitation wedding bells, Simon's mind rallied and he thought, 'Yes, she is beautiful, I will marry her. She will wear a silk dress and I'll buy her George Eliot's novels. We'll spend some time recovering from all this at Long Acre, and I'll tell her everything I've been through here and she will lie against the tree and listen, her huge eyes turned to mine, silently. But she'll be drinking it all in, and she will be good at not replying except in her gestures. And she will say quietly, "Come on Simon, let's go inside." And by that she will mean, 'I've heard everything and I understand.' And I shall walk behind her across the lawn through the French windows into the cool dark drawing room.' Then he remembered the smell of the upholstery and the jangling of the servants' bell and his mother's brown blotched hands, protruding veins and long fingers which had never painted or written except instructions for servants.

'We'll talk to my parents, but between the words we'll exchange glances and speak to each other in the silences, and then when mother goes out I will go to her...'

That was the scene he pictured, as his back was slapped affectionately, and it unfolded so easily in company. But when he was alone, particularly on watch, exhausted and cold - near the top of the list of war's horrors was the cold - at those times his imagination was not so fluent and his mind could not create an image of fulfilment. He realised that Lily's looks did not stir him, that the air between them was too easy and bland, and it hurt him to remember it. He began to dread being on watch.

He tried fighting these doubts, though he did not have much energy. He would begin with, 'It doesn't matter if I marry her or not. I could leave it.' This initial casualness was to ward off the strong 'no' of his instinct; to postpone the thought of separation and having to hurt her. His next tactic was to list the advantages (which was about as effective as a General formulating his strategies once the enemy has started to attack): 'She is the right one. I'll be thirty soon. When this wretched business is over I'll have to get a move on. After all she is waiting, ready and she is beautiful.' The last tactic, and the most likely to win in this state of sensual deprivation, was to picture her body. But invariably he would descend the dugout steps defeated, for though her body was fine, her delicately boned shoulders and small feet oddly poignant, they aroused in him none of the desperation that he had felt for the thirty-year old Annette whom he had met and loved in London. Yet it was Lily who pushed him to explore his mind; she who moved him towards a quality of thought which slovenly Annette numbed. When he remembered Annette he just wanted to eat.

Lily's letters cooled him. Reading them over and over by candlelight he tried to find in himself the rising to meet her but failed, for he balked at her neatness.

"My dear Simon (small round letters - too clean, too careful!),

I'm sending you this plus a food parcel knowing how awful it must be. I feel that to tell you what I am doing would be irrelevant to you. It would sound trivial compared to what you are going through, so I'll only write a little, and it will only be like a feather on water. But Simon come back soon. Please, please, come back soon..."

Her mention of irrelevance irritated him. She tried too hard. She knew more than most how this war opened a person and tore the lining out completely, she was sensitive, but behind her hundred or so sweet words, he felt her fingering his brain, seeking a power he could not give her. *He* was the poet not *her,* and 'feather on water' was his phrase. Her reticence and good manners were hiding an enormous demand.

He would turn then to his own writing and watch the words pour from him. He already had two small volumes of poetry published. Knowing that, whenever he saw him pad in hand, Frank, the cook, would move around him reverently, leaving a space that Lily never left. And because of that it was fox-faced Frank with tattooed arms that Simon wrote for, not beautiful Lily.

TO FRANK

The sea breaks soft on the sand.
Sand so soft it is barely land
And I just do not understand
How this earth, it works.

The shells break soft on the green
Shells so slow, each second is seen
And I know not any more what I mean
By the words I say.

The men march straight and slow
So calmly, so quietly they go
And I search their faces, trained not to show
The extent of the strength they have.

The war moves straight through its course
A war so planned that it needs no force
And I wonder why it is that I feel no remorse
For the things I have done.

My mind is frighteningly light
For a mind with death in sight
It's just I have not quite the might
To feel death is wrong.

Frank comes in, fresh clothes under arm
This day in the dugout's so calm
And I love him for this opiate balm
His routine pours over me.

(It's better by far
Than his tea.)

Simon had never written so much as he had in this last year. Previously there had been blanknesses, blockages, laziness, but now it had power. He could write about anything: landslides, aeroplanes, trees. It would come from his pen, not brilliantly but fast and easily.

And when he had read Lily's carefully constructed letters copied once, twice, three times he hastened to his pen as if to dodge an arrow that came to shatter the private treasure store inside him. In this sense she invoked his power, for her pursuit pushed him to withdraw; to find and consolidate his own resources.

She had always said, "Simon you are so clever. Simon, how do you know about that?" She would lean towards him not merely with affection, but as though to catch some of his knowledge. There was something crippled about her when she did this, he guiltily thought; something intensely weak and yet greedy. He did not like it, and it was at those times, her cheeks full and soft and her eyes wide, that he would turn away to conceal himself.

And now here he was standing in front of her, bleakly on the shingle. He turned to her and asked, "Shall we get married?"

She stopped dead, as if shot. Why had he said it? What had made him? It must have been fear, she supposed later, fear that she might have found someone else.

"Lily?" he asked again.

She did not move. They had walked miles along the beach. It was getting cold.

"Shall we go back?" she asked, as though he had not said anything. "It's getting late. Shall we go home?"

"Lily."

"I know." She put her hand on his arm to prevent his continuing. And her hand said, 'not yet, pretend you haven't said it, so I can think.'

"Please, let's just walk."

But the noise in his head was as loud as the sound of shells which used to wake him in France; or their phantom sounds here in peaceful Aldeburgh.

"Please Lily, hurry."

She seemed to be walking remarkably slowly, making much of the pebbles. At least they were not standing together in the drawing room, or she seated, her dark head towards the fire and he standing behind her, his hands on the sofa. It was easier outside.

He wondered what was happening inside her head, and thought how ridiculous it was that a lifetime should be clinched in a second. Why not sit down and write down the pros and cons? Why make it so suspended and dramatic?

She knew she was being dramatic, childish almost, but she couldn't help it any more than a toddler can explain a preference for orange over milk. It just knows what it wants, cries, grabs.

"Lily?"

"No," she said. "No, Simon." She was patient with her own simplicity.

His turn to be silent. He had never rehearsed a rejection. Never, despite the clarity of his war-time fears, had he visualised this scene as he had stood in the cold. He had always pictured fighting her off, gently, but sensitively, of course, sensitively. He would have to prize her mind away from his, suggest books for her to read, music for her to listen to, and then, in the wake of her gratitude, walk away.

Now she was saying no to him. He felt shaken, as if watching a building one has taken for granted as home falling before one's eyes. And as it did so, brick upon brick, he saw how fragile it had really been; those letters of hers how empty, not neat from wanting to please but neat from being stilted. She had constructed them as he had constructed her. Had he, self-absorbed, missed her real indifference along the way?

They both stopped walking, instinctively aware that now was the moment to speak and what had to be said must be pure and uninterrupted and they had to be looking at each other.

"Simon, there's something wrong." Again she could manage little more than approximations, but there was power under her awkwardness. She knew where she was going.

"I felt it a long time ago. Before you joined up. Do you remember that walk across Hound Tor and then our picnic?" She was recalling the scene in detail to cushion its point.

"You know, when I lost a shoe in the river and we slept under that rock that looked like an Eagle's head?"

Yes, of course he remembered.

"I knew it then. All day I felt it. It started as a kind of dryness. Then walking helped it." She was externalising the problem; strong enough to raise it but not to face it full on.

"Being out, free of Mummy and Iris for a while, that helped. But in the afternoon when we were resting, the feeling strengthened. Don't you remember my getting up suddenly and running down to the river saying I was going to get a drink and then throwing heather at you as though everything was all right? Don't you remember that? It was because I felt... under pressure, that we were pushing in the wrong direction."

Simon remembered too, differently, the birds swooping down on the river, the gathering cold at teatime and the message it had held. But he had been joining up a week later and so had not listened.

"It's a matter of incompatibility." She was fluent now because the bulk of the point had been made.

"I expect too much from you..." But she lost courage, did not know how to insult him with, "And you can't give it to me."

She could have added, "You haven't got it in you," but she was kinder and wiser than that, and for the freedom she desperately wanted, she was prepared to appear the loser.

For the first time she moved from his head into his body in a blaze that destroyed Annette and London completely. He had only been waiting for some fire in her: a raised voice, a single adamant retort in her own words rather than his merely returned or confirmed. That is all it would have taken, but coming out now in the night air as a steely refusal it was too late. He could have cried. Instead he put his hand on hers, then feeling her soft skin, clamped it desperately. It seemed an impertinence. More impertinent than a kiss. Hands are spirit; the mouth is body: red, wet, mammal.

She was less complete than he thought. For a second she caught fire too, but in the distance, cool water came, spreading through her as a permanence that flickering flames could never be. She was aware of the contrast, saw clearly the truth she sought though not where to get it. Misery and happiness collided in her, making her face rigid. Never mind. A path had opened.

Her misery was in seeing herself throwing away a life she had enjoyed, and also because it merited no word stronger than enjoyment. An image of spinsterhood came to her, cruelly vivid. Her mind quickly exaggerated it to punish herself for rejecting him. She mustered up thick stockings, ankle-less legs creeping into dress stores, obsessions. For a moment she could have said, "Yes, yes Simon. After you get back. Yes."

But her travelled soul pushed her away from compromise, and she took her hand from his. They resumed their walk to the end of the beach towards her expectant family who were drinking tea around the fire. They anticipated an announcement. The noise of the pebbles expressed the grating feelings which Simon had described well in

verse but never, until now, felt. The two were distressingly different.
   At the same time Lily felt the happiness of having made a stand. However awkwardly she had said it, she was clean.
   "I'll tell them," she said. "Afterwards, on their own. I'll explain." Simon was not so resolute. White embers stirred in him. For the first time he felt afraid of going back to France: no promise as company (as a poet promises were more potent than their realisation); no slap of congratulation on his jacketed back.
   Reaching the gate, lights on in the sitting room, music summoning them, he was reminded that it had never been his intention to propose. Why had he done it? The mystery absorbed his sadness. It gave Lily space to move towards him.
   "I shall write," she smiled.
   Simon turned to her amazed. He was a deep man, but narrow when it came to convention. Women were either yours or they were not.

   Dear Simon,

   It's an amazing winter here. I've never known it so cold. I get up an hour later just to avoid it. Mother is sweeping the snow from the drive. She doesn't know I'm awake yet, and I suddenly felt like writing, so I'll let her think I'm asleep. She knows I'm lazy anyway. I've been thinking of perhaps spending some more time here when Mummy and Daddy return to London. On my own. Not that I don't like being with them, I just want to be on my own. I think they'll understand, they're remarkable people. They don't ask questions, just support, even though I shan't be following the little path they must have mapped out for me. Sometimes I feel depressed about that. But I can't help knowing that life won't be ordinary, although it's like digging for something, I don't know what!
   Anyway, how are you? Silly question. It must still be awful. And it all seems to have gone on so long. Mother has knitted you a jumper. Will you be allowed to wear it under your jacket? I know they're strict about those things which seems ridiculous when people are

dying all around you. Oh God, she's calling me.

Never had she been so spontaneous. The move from romance to friendship made her words gentle not incisive. She wanted him to be well. Before, she had just wanted him.

When Simon read the letter - two pages longer, in writing that sloped easily across the page - he imbibed the gentleness, was warmed. He was sitting with Frank at the time. Eternal Frank. And the warmth stretched out to touch the pinched, fox face of this man who had frozen himself up with dutifulness. The warmth was shared as friendship not passion can be.

It gave them both what they needed. Flames would have been too strong. Sunshine was better. Simon missed sun; sun and space and solitude. It seemed never to be day here and when it was, it was too hot, sticky hot, because of the heavy uniform and the work. Tramping around, digging, pushing as one body through the mud of the trenches.

"Lily, Lily, Lily."

That night Simon tried to find Lily's form and face, but she was not there. Instead there was still the warmth, so different from the loneliness he had expected. He used it to get him up the next morning and climb the steps to the men who had been up all night and were frozen with physical and emotional seizure. It made fat his 'Good morning'.

Lily was sitting in the morning room, wondering whether she should continue writing to Simon. She did not want to hold him any more, yet she still did not quite appreciate her release. Head on her cardiganed arms, she felt she had cut off a source of energy which had buoyed life up. And looking out onto the wild stretch of green that was their garden, she could not see anything to feel about.

The path had been special because they had strolled up it, one behind the other. The apple tree had her affection because they had lain under it. This room with its wooden dresser, blue and white cups hanging diagonally, yellow curtains, was cosy because they had burst into it from the cold. Images of them being together here had long since overlaid the easy peace of her childhood memories. And now she had to rid the place of him, because she could not draw on the association once the relationship was dead.

And what else was there? The confident warmth of her letter had been true, but underneath it there was an enormous blankness, for her 'no' to Simon was a 'no' to birth upon birth of dependence; of living comfortably, entangled, double.

Lily stayed often in her room writing, or else walked alone. Her quietness was a puzzle to her parents; a jut into the cosiness of their private pursuits: father, his book on the Punic Wars; mother, her secretarial pension-fund scheme for disabled soldiers. And it was the more pronounced for there normally being no thread between the two adults to tug at their concentration.

In the time to come, her thoughts would abstractedly seek Simon. Her mind filtered his weaknesses and she just saw his fine hands, his broad back and intelligent face.

"Married a woman from Chelsea five years older than him - clever - though apparently he doesn't write any more poetry," a friend told her six months later, as they had tea and meringues in a local tea shop. There was a powerful pang as the meringue turned to dust in her throat, but it was brief like the end of a fever.

It was the end of the war. Lily was treading new ground, though she continued to walk the same stretch of beach. The ruin she had peered into a thousand times, seeking treasure in its dark corners, dirtying her gloves as she fingered the moss on its walls, was the same ruin. But it was different now and different sea lapped her booted feet.

This newness was a little frightening, but the rightness of her decision supported her. She could have walked miles, stayed up all night, said anything to anyone.

She began to move between extremes - formality and lightness, knowing that the first was protecting a new Lily. New. New. New. The words exhilarated her, as she imagined well-turned phrases might have done Simon.

She needed an anchor though. Someone to tell her where she was going. On one of her walks, she felt too light, like a disembodied spirit above and outside her body. Though an old couple stepping out for a stroll - their retirement years rejuvenated by the relief of being too old for war - registered her as a young figure in blue, whose hand went now and then to her broad-rimmed hat the wind was threatening to carry out to sea.

PADMA

As a mark of respect
they fenced him off,
his uniqueness a kind of penance.

She needed an anchor though. Someone to tell her where she was going...

When Padma heard that her mother's brother had died she felt a weakness in her head that even months afterwards, the mourning complete, domestic routine resumed, made her say to her little sister, "No Asha, I'm not coming to the pool today," or "Ma, why not give the visitors plain roti instead of panni. Does it matter? They won't mind..."

"Padma, that is not good enough. They are our friends. What's the matter with you?" Her mother, stressed by the pressures of serving her husband and raising a family on little money, turned Padma's petulance into an issue which it was, but neither of them knew it then.

In the night, she had seen her daughter's wedding; the fireworks, the jewellery; had planned the food, the sweets; picturing it all in the Narayan temple. It would actually be in the local temple and afterwards in their own home, but her sleepy mind took it to a setting where there was colour and honour. And she had thanked Shiva that her Padma was beautiful and healthy and so helpful to her.

Yet lately she had not been. Her face was still beautiful, but there was a sulkiness in it which made her mother check before asking her to fetch water or roll chapattis. And why did she look so tired? For a mother, still responsible for her daughter's body, that was the hardest to take. She watched her carrying Kapil; saw how she struggled with his weight and how, putting him down, her arms seemed thin and her back not as straight as it had been. It was difficult to see under her punjabi top if she had lost weight, but Ma suspected that she had.

"Take her to see Doctor Mitra," her husband suggested. "He's an understanding man. Maybe he will prescribe a tonic."

Ma sat in the small waiting room looking at the posters on its walls which recommended a vegetarian diet and advised inoculations against cholera. And she wondered whether Kapil needed any more jabs. He was sitting on the floor playing with an abacus sent by her brother-in-law, a successful businessman in Jaipur.

Doctor Mitra, an Anglo-Indian who, as some people unkindly remarked, spoke Hindi with an English accent looked at Padma, Parker 60 balanced between right index finger and thumb while his left finger pulled at Padma's lower eyelid.

"I don't know what it is, Doctor, but I'm feeling unwell, yet I am not. And the tiredness... it doesn't get better with sleep." She wanted to tell him what it was like being the elder girl in the family, but loyalty and the suspicion that it was irrelevant to this grey exhaustion, kept her quiet.

"You are anaemic," he said. "Take a rest from household duties and try this tonic. Let me know how you get on."

"Your tonic won't help me, Doctor," Padma said forcefully. "It's my mind that is hurting."

"Ah, you have a psychosomatic disorder." This particular word was a recent acquisition and, liking it, it cropped up often in his advice to patients though it did not affect his pill-happy approach to treatment. He either overlooked his patients' minds completely, or suggested, for instance, that the reason for a plain cough suffered by a seventy year old mataji, was fear of death.

"It is as though a weight is pulling me down," she pursued, not understanding.

"Padma, I wonder if you should go to see a brahmin priest?" he suddenly suggested. "He could perhaps give you some good advice."

"You mean it is my mind that is ill, Sir? You mean your tonic won't work?" She was half disappointed for, despite her resistance, she had subconsciously planned to place her hopes in the bottle; to sit it on the stool in her room and take it as directed.

"I mean that the tonic may help your body, but this little difficulty you have (he always said 'little' when dealing with something ambiguous) should be referred to someone of a spiritual nature. I myself am not... well, never mind." He was hungry and disentangling causes took time.

Ma was summoned. Dr Mitra discussed the referral briefly, and Ma, programmed for obedience, agreed.

The priest's room was a small one behind the temple. As he spent most of his time in the vastness of the temple itself, surreptitiously considering it not only to be the territory of the gods but also his own, he was satisfied with a relatively small personal space.

"Yes, what is it?" he asked amiably.

Ma was sensible enough to have her daughter speak for herself though she remained present for she had heard stories about brahmin priests.

"It's my mind. It hurts," said Padma.

"These things come as tests to our strength, Padma. You are young, but remember: as a reincarnated soul you may carry many burdens from the past, and when these are about to be taken from you they come with force to say good-bye."

"What should we do then?" Ma thought him sensible but wanted practical advice; and in the 'we', automatically assumed her part in the child's cure.

"She should spend more time in worship, for worship accumulates power in the soul. And when there is power in the soul it can face these little things." The 'little' linked the priest with the doctor, and Padma distrusted his advice, although he may have been right.

"I suggest you worship Sanjay, the God of Light. Make him an offering, and he will help you face whatever is troubling you."

The priest began to feel uneasy. Confident in his own judgement, he knew when he was on the wrong track. His conscience was dead to greed, yet it had a flapping alertness to misjudgement.

"In addition," he went on, "I suggest you go to visit Bhagirath. He is experienced in these matters, and is here in Calcutta at present. My area is strictly methods of worship. I do not go into these mental complications for they distract me from my work. He might be able to help you though."

The concession to Bhagirath was a generous one considering the priest was jealous. Bhagirath had had visions and seemed to be breaking new ground spiritually. But Padma's face, open, questioning and a touch fierce had made him say it. They thanked him and left.

"I don't want to see Bhagirath, Ma," Padma whined, her shoulders drooping. "I've had enough. I'll just try to get better with Dr Mitra's tonic." Ma was reluctant too, uncomfortable in matters beyond her understanding. But she had worked herself up and could not simply do nothing.

Dressed in a fresh sari she went to the temple. She was normally negligent in this, considering her family duties to be sufficient proof of her devotion, yet this time she had clearly failed to elicit the help of the gods.

In a corner a brahmin priest sat eating prasad. Incense wisped into the heavy air. She prayed to Lord Sanjay for half an hour and felt better as she lifted her large behind off the floor and rustled her sari back into pleats; the kind of 'better' one feels after carrying out instructions. She was a bit afraid of her indifference to religious matters and so, walking to catch a rickshaw, she concocted a meagre experience out of the fusion of impressions; something her head could return to for solace. She was not planning upon regular visits.

It was about as powerful as the tonic which had as intended become a source of reassurance to Padma's conscious mind; the part which connected with speech and furrowed brow. The small improvement helped her to stay quiet and her face filled out enough to waylay Ma's anxiety.

"You do look better," Dr Mitra said, passing her in the street as she was fetching ginger and potatoes; her routine, despite his advice, having changed very little. Had she looked worse, he would either have noticed something on the other side of the street or glared at her heavy bag as if to say, 'So Padma, you didn't take my advice and look at you now.' But as she looked well, he took the credit.

Actually she was worse. She was deeply troubled by the sensations of weakening which were no longer a vague wash of feeling but an exact series of attacks that seemed to fall on certain days at certain times. She started to take note of it and to prepare herself in a way someone much older, more experienced, may not have thought to do. And because of her strategy and her strengthened face, she could sustain her policy of silence towards her mother who was anyway more concerned these days with the arrival of a third child.

Yet it was lonely working against this turmoil she did not understand. And the loneliness interfered with light-hearted pursuits and made social occasions more to be prepared for than enjoyed. She had followed the brahmin's advice and had been to worship Sanjay several times. But a statue could not speak, could not put its arm round her and say, 'Padma, it will be all right.' No, a statue could not help her; however sweet its face; however adorned with flowers and gifts.

That year her body strengthened as the effort required to prepare for these private onslaughts manifested in muscle power. This made it less feasible to explain, for few understood that if the body is strong, the mind is not necessarily.

It was November: her birthday. Dr Mitra came. Aunt Susmita came and all her cousins too. Her father wore a new shirt which he had had unopened in his cupboard for several months. But the party had caused tension in Padma's mind because it was on such family occasions that she felt most vulnerable. She had made all the preparation she could: a ritual of silence, a slowing of her breath, a controlling of her thoughts, a withdrawal; as a person might tidy and lock everything away before going out so that in the streets, shopping, talking, partying they will not be afraid to return to a ransacked house.

But when she walked into the front room and they were all there, so affectionate and relaxed, the last step in the procedure failed her and they flooded in. It was her birthday after all. At any other time it would have been fine. And by all normal standards of affection it *was* fine: they loved her, she them; they were colourful, cheerful, relaxed and she the centre of their happy attention. But just now she was following another line - distinct from the heart line - and its gradual appearance in her mind was absorbing her; as the birth of a baby might absorb a mother and distance her from news of world events. It was no one's fault, but Padma felt their jollity, their endless movement, particularly their enquiries after her health, distressing.

She sought the large comfort of her aunt Susmita who somehow steadied the leap of her mind. The movement was an attempt to keep in tact the process which ordinariness and the quiet completion of her duties normally protected. Susmita was chewing on a puri.

"Padma, what is the matter? You look strange."

"I am all right."

She was sitting on the arm of Susmita's chair. Her mind did a flip inwards: became careful, controlled.

'What are you doing there?' she accused the feeling inside; the thief of her normal adolescence. 'Why's this happening to me?' It was the first time she had really asked; the first time she had not panicked, taken measures and just got by. Seated in the unthreatening calmness of her aunt's company - her aunt who had not the capacity to understand exactly but who had a quality of fat protectiveness - there was a shift. She took time to look.

'My niece is over-excited. It is the change of weather. I am glad I don't live in this Calcutta,' Susmita thought, her bare arm resting heavily on Padma's shoulder. Curiously, under this stabilising weight, more real than any waft of insight from a temple visit and more innocent, Padma relaxed. Susmita's thoughts had wandered away from her niece to her home and her renovation plans, and so Padma had just the arm and not the woman. And resting in it, she was able to glimpse the good side of her tension. It was like seeing the hidden advantage in having an irritating friend whose presence serves to increase one's resilience and patience.

Yes, Padma had learned quietness from her difficulty. And watching the careless romping of her cousins who seemed aware of nothing much more than touch and taste and colour, she was grateful. Next to them she felt very old.

One day, out of the blue, Ma's brother-in-law, the businessman, sent money for the family to go on holiday, to have a break from Calcutta.

"Why not go into the hills," he wrote, "spend a few weeks...?"

Padma had been indifferent about going, as though her old soul knew that a change of location was irrelevant to an internal illness; that it either suppressed it, or worse, made it more delicate, or even - 'Please, no' - intensified it as the body had to cope with a new environment.

Amidst all the hustle - Ma sweating fat in the queue to book the tickets, whilst Bap finished his accounts, explaining to his partner what was left to do, about who might come to the office and how they might be helped - they had forgotten that the small town they were going to, known by a few in Calcutta as a honeymoon resort, was where Bhagirath lived in his ashram.

But it was exciting travelling by train; Sanjay, sleepless and noisy, crawling across the dusty seats to a lawyer who was trying to relax, being slapped by Ma and made to sit heavy in her lap; Kapil, listless yet talkative; Bap, patient and silent; and Padma, looking out of the window at the scrub, at villagers ambling, water pots on their heads or crouching in noisy bunches at the stations into which the train clanked again and again through the evening and night.

On the third evening of their stay, Ma and Padma found themselves strolling past the white buildings of the ashram while Bap,

Kapil and Sanjay were resting. Ma suggested they go in and have a look. It had been mentioned in the hotel and lying in the heat of the early afternoon, her sari folded over the back of the chair, cold tea on the table beside her, Ma had thought: 'Why not go for a walk there!'

It took her to thinking of Padma, neglected lately, partly because of her fattened face and partly because of new concerns about Sanjay's sores. She touched the merged strangeness in the girl; knew with a frightening, quick clarity that whatever had been happening to her daughter was still happening.

Bhagirath was in the courtyard sitting on a stone flag outside the visitor's room, its green curtain flapping gently in the six o'clock breeze. It was unusual for him to be there and more unusual for him to be alone. They approached him, curious and respectful.

A tall man obviously, though it was not clear quite how tall; an old man too, though seeing his fine face it was not clear quite how old.

"He looks so healthy," whispered Ma, health on her mind. "Do you think he's seen us?"

He had. He got up, put his palms together and greeted them as though their arrival were an occasion. Or was he always like that, always gracious? Extraordinarily, without hesitation, he asked them if they would like tea as if to friends he had been expecting and, judging from the speedy arrival of tray, cups, sweets, had planned for. They sat stiffly and a little confused in the small room the green curtain had concealed; not aware that he usually left the task of welcoming visitors to others. He asked them what they were doing here, whether it was a holiday, how the train journey had been, again as though this, not the small hotel by the lake, had been their destination.

Padma sat to his left on the bench. It was a bit dark in the room but refreshingly so after the glare of the white buildings. She had been fine since they arrived; had been wrong about the change of environment; it had helped, even to the point of forgetting, as they strolled around the lake, watching the women washing their clothes, hearing the sannyasis' bell in the distance.

Meeting Bhagirath... now she remembered! Because in the darkened room, the weakness came. She withdrew, checked, quietened and then something strange: he offered more biscuits, continued to chat, was not even facing Padma, yet seemed to be speaking to her, mind to mind, with an affection almost too intense to withstand this continued tea-time ordinariness.

"I've been waiting for you," he said. "I've been waiting for you. You should have come sooner."

A woman stopped by, pulling aside the edge of the curtain. He invited her in as if she were part of his private explanation. The woman sat down and started to talk to them about the ashram, how it had begun, what they did here and so on, but first she invited them to observe a moment of silence, that was so silent it was frightening. Padma looked enquiringly at Ma, who had her eyes shut, and then back to the woman. She couldn't take her eyes off her. Her face began to burn and she knew, as clearly as one recognises someone whose journey has followed similar tracks, that what the woman was doing in the silence was what she, Padma, had been doing for all those months alone: withdrawing, checking, watching. Tears welled up behind her attentive eyes. She knew it was important to remain composed, but when the woman filled the silence with a businesslike explanation of their beliefs, the contrast hurt her and she made her eyelids soft shields against her breaking.

The woman's voice, too cool for what she was talking about, absorbed her mother. Padma could feel Ma's nodding, smiling head. Responding to her interest, the woman spoke to Ma alone.

And alone too, for the women's conversation allowed privacy, Bhagirath addressed Padma. Silently. For how can words speak intimacy to a stranger?

"You could have come sooner. Did you not hear the signal? Did you not hear what the priest said? Your mind must move at the slightest call, so that even thousands of miles away you can receive help or warning. One day you will be far away. Will you hear then?"

Then he paused as their bodies moved across the silence to put cup to mouth and he to hand Ma more tea. He was so respectful she noticed, as though drinking the tea were as important as what he was saying to her in the silence.

They settled. Cup went back to tray. Ma resumed her attentive stance, the woman pointed... Padma panicked. Did that mean they would get up, go away? Please no, for there was more to be said, wasn't there? Bhagirath's thoughts entering her were like water gulped after weeks of thirst. And he, with his politeness, was inviting her to sip as though it were tea not love she were drinking, as though there were no hurry, which there wasn't for him because he understood eternity.

She wanted to shout, to be spontaneous and affectionate, for this little room was a destination, but her body was clamped in polite torpor.

Ma stood up and took her hand. Bhagirath smiled, shook hands, expressing nothing more than cool friendliness; a duty done; and even as he turned to Padma extending his hand for the third time, it seemed a routine gesture; no sign whatever of what had been exchanged. She was confused and wanted to ask him to speak out loud. Instead he turned to Ma with reverence. And miraculously Padma understood: parents should be respected and intimacy, spoken in words, would be in some way an insult.

Walking past the white-washed buildings, taking in nothing, concealing herself behind her mother's chatter, she searched back to when she first started to have her strange experiences and she realised why the death of her uncle had had such an impact on her. He had been young and kind, and the injustice of his illness had pounded at her brain and made it fragile. In turn, the fragility had cleansed her, for it had forced reserve and caution upon her. She had started to question life, and though her body moved through the same daily routine, what she was discovering in her mind felt more real. The words that had come to her just now, across the peaceful little room, connected with that reality like two beads of the same necklace clicking together on their string. It was a separate world she had touched, yet judging from Bhagirath's good tea-time manners and his deep, observant eyes, one could evidently live in both worlds at once. A fact that many who lived with him still found hard to grapple with. The discovery, as yet unarticulated in her head, exhilarated her, and she skipped ahead of her parents as they went back to the hotel. They concluded that the visit had bored her, that she was glad to be away.

A year later the news came on thin sheets of paper from which her mother read as they sat eating, that Susmita was suffering from high blood pressure and had been recommended a change of air. And Padma knew, as though she were simply remembering an incident that had happened before, that all the right people would say the right things at the right time to lead Susmita to the ashram with Padma as her guide; for Padma would plead and plead with the remains of a power which had always won her what she had wanted.

So eighteen months after the original visit, under the fat arm of her aunt, covered now because it was winter and trusted because it was an aunt's; a balanced Hindu woman's arm, Padma rested in the long train journey from Calcutta to a station in Rajasthan whose name she had forgotten. When she had visited it before, her mind not her eyes had been alert.

Susmita went to get better and Padma went to stay. If she did not, there was a boy two streets away waiting to marry her and Ma was already planning the fireworks. Padma wanted the truth she had seen in Bhagirath. And she knew with the certainty of one who has finally found what they are looking for that Susmita would back her up; would persuade Ma and Bap that this was what she must do. And the force that would compel the woman would also heal her.

At twenty-two Padma was still with Bhagirath, accompanying him as closely and often as his love for solitude would allow. Superficially it was his oldness - he was eighty-three - that made this pursuit of intimacy different from previous ones she had sought. In reality what distinguished it was that the more she was with him the more she felt alone with herself. He had a dignity that made intimacy a means of clarifying not losing herself. She could learn from him how to enjoy being alone in the atmosphere of her own spirit without being forced there by rejection. And he left no one bereft, for his white-clad body, moving silently around the buildings, seemed to fill automatically the spaces made by uncertainties. He was there but he was not there.

One day he gave her the ladle to churn the butter. It banged against the side of the stone pot. He took it from her and demonstrated, his old arms strong and rhythmic. But again the ladle slipped and butter splattered onto her face and pinafore. She wiped it off and shrugged, giving up. He placed her small hands a third time on the ladle and then put his own on top of them. They churned together and she felt a power move through her fingers. Her hands seemed as strong and as firm as his and her body stood solid. The butter firmed and they gathered the bits from around the edge of the pot, scooping them into a ball - nothing should be wasted. In that last easy stage he loosened his grip. The last part of the job she must do alone. She faltered, paused, then understanding him, lifted the ladle to catch the last scrap which was about to drip over the edge and skilfully joined it to the whole. One last step remained; to pound the butter flat. He lifted his hands away completely. She hit at the yellow ball and flattened it. Enjoying the smack of the ladle, she hadn't noticed he had walked away. Beside her was Meera, the cook, holding out a plate, smiling.

Meera was older than Padma but she was one of her closest friends. She seemed to take life less seriously; to forget if she made a mistake while Padma worried about everything; she so wanted to please, and particularly Bhagirath who was perfection itself. Meera loved him too, but not obsessively. Hers was a tempered passion, for he was a holy man, not God.

He was standing in a doorway, white on white wall. Padma approached him wanting to be close for she could feel his slipping away down the road to death. He did not see her. His eyes rested lightly on the jagged ridge of mountains that surrounded the ashram.

"Bhagirath," she said softly.

He did not seem to hear.

Again: "Bhagirath, don't go, please." Her body was filled with a violence of feeling that was so different from his quietness that she was ashamed of it. He said nothing but turned back into the doorway and disappeared. She was angry. 'Why doesn't he care? Why is he so distant and cold?' This situation recurred again and again because silent love was such a foreign language to her; the language of that other disconnected world which she had touched and wanted but could not fully inhabit. She suspected his aloofness was taking her closer to it. But she needed confirmation though that would be self-defeating because it would make her lazy. Sometimes it was all a little too hard, this subtle love, and she would remember her mother bounding through the doors, uninvited, to check if she was well. She had resented the heaviness of her step then, and did not want it now, but she missed its ease.

Her feet punished the ground as she marched away, sat on the stone wall outside the kitchen as far away from the calmness she learned here as was her mother who banged plates in the sink and shouted at adolescent Kapil. And she cried. An old woman cutting coriander on the step looked up, smiled a toothless smile and then resumed. Padma was angry with her too: 'Why doesn't she come to me at least?' But the woman was a monument of peace and did not break her rhythm for the sake of a few tears.

Bhagirath lay on his bed, her hurt unfelt. His spirit was too far away to feel any violence. He died.

Messages, telegrams, flowers, sandalwood, a pyre. They stood around the body of flowers. Padma looked down to conceal her red eyes. Meera called her quietly to come and throw petals. It made her jump and she slipped on some oil as she joined them. Meera steadied her and a line of love, like the thread in a rosary, passed through them as the group watched her recover herself. They knew how much she had loved Bhagirath and her love joined theirs, making them one force. Carefully they passed her sandalwood and jasmine. It reminded her of the way Bhagirath had passed her mother tea that first day and she realised that this life would go on; that this love could not be burnt by a fire. For why would they be building the pyre with so much care if it were to destroy what they cherished? Still she cried, but her tears were cooler.

Three days after the fasting was over, Padma asked Meera if she could be given the duty of churning the butter.

STEVEN

The lively orange tree
wanted to bear fruit
but the climate was wrong.

This situation occurred again and again because silent love was such a foreign language to her; the language of that other disconnected world which she had touched and wanted but could not fully inhabit...

His mother had not wanted him to go though she had not said so. But she had lost sleep over it and twice asked for his flight number which he duly wrote on the back of a cab card picked up from the hall mat.
"It'll be fine, Mum. Besides, I'm with two friends. We'll be careful."
"Yes." She was beating an egg - extremely hard, he thought - and he was hit by a childish urge to make faces at her back because she always saw the snags in things. Instead she turned and asked him to fetch the milk from the fridge. He saw the effort she was making to hide her worry and sorry, he passed it to her as though it were flowers.
They ate dinner together, interrupted only by a phone call from Patrick checking that everything was all right and that Steven would meet them at the Qantas check-in counter at ten the next morning. Jenny resisted the temptation to ask him what Patrick had said and continued to be jolly about the chance of seeing the pyramids and going down the Nile.
Later that night she slipped some mosquito cream into a side pocket of his rucksack. It was the next best thing to putting food there. Something for his body at least. The food was so bad in Cairo, they had told her. Cooked on street corners. Dirty. And where would he sleep, travelling around like that?
"Mum, it will be all right," he said as he lugged the rucksack down the stairs the next morning. Refreshed from sleep and the knowledge that he would be away in an hour or so, the words carried a different message from the evening before. She had always said that

if an angel could speak it would say: 'It will be all right.' Steven was not bad but he was no angel; and those fellows he had chosen to go with even less so. At least they were physically strong and could defend themselves. Steven was thin and so stupid sometimes. I mean, my God, what about the time he went by train all the way up to Broken Hill when he should have been heading for Bourke!

"Why not go to Europe, Steven? What about Greece?" she said in a last ridiculous bid as he gulped down a cup of cold tea.

"We are going to Egypt," he remarked simply, stuffing a water bottle with his free hand into the pocket with the mosquito cream in it. Too lazy to take everything out of the pocket and pack it properly, he did not see the cream. He would find it in a quiet moment, kneeling on a hotel floor in the heat and smell of dust and incense and be grateful.

Jenny stood at the door, still in her housecoat, as he got into the taxi which was driven by a young Asian whom she rather wished were Steven for he would be home at the end of his working day, watching television with a tray of supper on his knees.

When he had gone she wheeled in the green dustbins and phoned to confirm her hair appointment for Denise's party.

"Best just get on. He'll be all right." The words carried a power.

She did things to the house that morning that she never usually did. She cleared out Steven's room, even considered painting it as she stood there with a windcheater in her hand, picked up his books, piled them into corners and went out shutting the door, everything settled. The house she had shared with him on and off for twenty-one years was now totally hers.

Still in her housecoat, she began re-lining the saucepan cupboard, regressing in her head to a period in Steven's life when such an activity would have been a waste of time, for he used to have an obsession with scrunching up paper as though to stoke a fire. He hadn't done that for years, obviously, but it now seemed worth the effort to do the job properly. She had a nice roll of paper in the other cupboard, the one they called 'Ted' because Ted, a man from town, had made it.

'Why am I doing this?' she wondered at about eleven-thirty.

'Why am I behaving as though he is dead? Why am I getting so obsessive? I've got to be ready by one.' But she couldn't stop.

Through and through each room she went as though wanting to lift a layer of his presence which her looking not her cloth could erase. She kept talking to herself: 'Come on Jenny, that's enough.' And then sipping coffee from a thick-rimmed mug, she would be up again to look.

By twelve-thirty she was sitting on her bed. She needn't have worried about the time. Instinctively she had known it had been important to go through all that and anyway she never took long to get ready. Now that the house was in order she was even quicker, because her mind was light and directioned, having shed with a strange ease the pain Steven's casual preparations and departure had caused her.

The party - only a lunch - was suddenly important. She enjoyed the quietness in a way that she often had not when Steven was away at university. She put on her dress. It was old but it felt good because of the house. Her body was aligned and cool. She knew that for the rest of the day she needn't think. She would just speak and it would be all right. She could judge by the way the coat hangers did not snarl up.

She drove down Longcombe Street, away from the house in which Steven, as a baby, had screamed so loudly that the Residents Association had mentioned, politely because she had no husband, that perhaps she should request the advice of a Health Counsellor. Her baby had not wanted to be in that house; had destroyed her sleep for three years. But once he had grown into a little boy and could be spoken to face to face rather than to a bundle whose absent personality frightened her, and explained to that sleep wasn't frightening, he seemed to settle down. Then he went through a period of insatiable greed so that, entering his bedroom, she had to climb over the mountain of possessions he had built around him. And when she touched them, he hit her as though these odds and ends, meagre enough to her - embarrassing even, when certain relations came - were gold to her child. 'As though he's come to me from a monastery, or somewhere,' she had thought.

Her hair cut in a new style, she drove down the avenue to the party, to where the flowers grew in orange equidistant bunches, and experienced the pleasure of being on neutral ground. It was not a place she would have chosen: crazy paving, plastic window boxes, large - almost obscenely large - roses, but she could enjoy it, for it had nothing to do with her. The immaculate rockery in her own garden depressed her each time she saw it because it was always 'to do' like the hedge trimming, bulb planting, lawn cutting. Jenny found life a burden. It was good, therefore, to hear the unthinking reassurances about Steven offered by acquaintances: "Don't worry, Jenny. When John went on his trip round Afghanistan, he nearly had to eat human flesh, and now look how strong and healthy he is."

"Yeah, but now he's a vegetarian!" someone joked, to uproarious laughter.

And when Andrew, a forty-nine year old banker she had known for several years, leant forward and suggested that she should take up painting again, she thought, 'Yes, that's true. It's good to work with colours, to dabble around - maybe sell one or two.' And because of his voice and well-formed face she forgot her frustration at being a bad draughtsman and remembered only the colours and the arty feel of the painting smock that made her look younger and more relaxed.

"You've got a real talent there." He was encouraging like a woman and as though she were a real concern of his; which for a moment she was because he was admiring her feline nose and strong chin. 'And she is a kind woman. Back's a little stooped, but what's that!' his mind continued. 'Besides, my back's a killer, especially on Sundays doing that garden.'

"Nice garden, isn't it?" he said, as though the view beyond Jenny's nose had initiated the thought.

"Yes, lovely," she agreed. And in their agreement they met, more intimately than before, as if she were free of an insecurity that had made dresses droop on her, made her palms damp and the pizza sag in the oven.

"Mum, not again."

"Oh, Steven, sorry."

"Sokay, I'll mash it."

Denise's egg rolls were compact. Jenny and Andrew met in those too; in the holding of them, the chewing of them, the standing in the same spot of sunlight through the trees, as on a stage.

And when everyone else went swimming, he told her the details of his divorce. 'He wants my sympathy,' she thought, and because they had been standing opposite each other for quite some moments in exactly the same position, her thought reached him complete. He shifted, put a foot forward, said, "But you don't want to hear about this," which she did, but not manipulatively, for it made him pathetic and she did not want him like that.

Her thoughts became mixed as they ate a little more egg. But they still stayed and watched the youngsters in the pool while others bunched together in the sunshine. Someone dropped a glass and Denise rushed for a cloth. They were compelled to watch because they had nothing left to say unless they addressed each other directly. And that would now be difficult. So they concentrated on the broken glass and hoped it would take a long time to pick up which it did because it is hard to find glass in the grass. Then when finally Denise's daughter, Sandra, entertained the guests with a dance, they met again, for both considered it rather unsavoury to parade one's child at parties. And they stayed in tune for as long as it took Sandra to complete her number - which was quite some time because she mistook the kind claps for an encore.

Not yet adjusted to life in Egypt, Steven sat outside the Kebab House in a Cairo main street thinking, 'I suppose it's all right to eat this beanburger.'

He didn't want to make a fuss. The other two, legs stretched out, were relaxed about it and ate fast. He was unsure. It was so cheap and the cook's hands looked as though he had been crawling on the road. He noticed that his own were not much better.

"Come on, Steve, it's fine."

His concern then transferred to where they would sleep. The hotel they had found above the raging night club only had two beds left.

"I'll go back to the hostel," he said. "You two can stay here and I'll meet you in the morning. I'll get a taxi."

"Good on ya, Steve," they said, appreciating his generosity but thinking him a bit stupid for offering. Still, he'd been a bit odd since they had arrived.

At university they were just drinking friends and the decision to come to Egypt had been a quick one, yet strangely it had stuck. The other two were enjoying themselves; liked the smells, the noise, the constant humping of rucksacks and hanging off buses. But Steven was feeling dislocated and didn't dare say so.

He had felt disorientated at the pyramids. People had hassled them for money. It had been hot and the Sphinx's head aroused sensations in him which had clashed with the smell, the red lemonade, the dreams he had had in the early morning. And that dog image, that

Anubis, that seemed to be everywhere...
He did not want to go to a night club that evening.
"Why not?"
His snaky back humped and he wiped his nose with the back of his hand.
"Just don't feel like it."
"Okay then. Well, guess we'll see you tomorrow around eight. We'll have to start early for Luxor."
He was cross that they assumed he had agreed on what would be a day's hot journey by train. But he would go because he could not make decisions in Cairo. It was too ragged and stifling. At home in his room, in front of a book, turning pages slowly, calculator there, cup of tea on the enamel coaster, he was clear. Here everything was dog-eared and entangled.
"All right then, see you tomorrow."
"You all right to get a taxi then?"
"Yeah, 'course. Have fun."
They had taken taxis before, knew how to refuse outrageous charges. His galabaya - they had bought them for fun - was dragging on the pavement. He let it.
He beckoned a taxi, got in, waved. They returned the wave and resumed planning. Steven felt lonely. Egypt was very lonely. It was only then he noticed he was in the front seat. He had always sat in the front as a boy. As an only child it was automatic. All his life he had sat in the front seat. Maybe he was seeking the company.
"Never sit in the front seat of a taxi," his mother had once said.
The taxi driver was speaking fast and driving fast. What the hell was the youth hostel called? He could not remember, so he said youth hostel twice as though speaking to a deaf man. The man nodded. He had understood. He turned on some music, looked cheerful. Steven began to relax. The man seemed to be going in the right direction. Fast though. Long time though? Half an hour about, must be. The place closes at eleven, doesn't it?
They had eaten late because they had watched the sunset at Giza as Pete's aunt had suggested. It must be at least a quarter-to by now. It was taking too long.
"Where are you going?"
The man didn't understand. Just lifted his hand as though to say, 'Don't tell me my job.' Pete had said it would only take fifteen

minutes. The driver started singing to the music, hitting his knee. Steven wished he wouldn't, wished he'd hurry up. He was reminded of being lost in a supermarket and a man lifting him high into the air, talking to him, carrying him to the till. He wished for that cosy rescue now.

"Hurry up," he said blankly to the man or the car or the situation, hardly audible above the cheap engine and the music. "Hurry up, or the place will close."

They seemed to be going over a bridge.

'We shouldn't be going over a bridge. Definitely not.' There was a distinct sense now that the man was heading nowhere in particular. He was still singing.

Abruptly the man stopped the car, turned off the headlights, switched on the interior light. He swivelled round towards Steven as though settling.

'What? What...'

He put his hand in his pocket. Steven knew, as one knows things that are meant to be surprises, that there was a knife in the pocket. The man did not get it out. Instead his hand still in the pocket held the knife tightly.

Jenny was slicing fruit. It was early morning. She was wondering whether or not to agree to Andrew's offer of dinner which, being forty-two, she knew meant more than dinner. What would Steven think? Would he mind? Her head tightened. She felt tired. Then quickly and clearly a thought intervened: 'He's twenty-one. I'm free.' And she took her hand off her son for the first time in twenty years.

Steven knew at that split second exactly what was intended: the knife would be into him, his money purse taken - 'No Steven, get this one with the buckle. Velcro won't last. I'll pay the extra,' his mother had said.

The Nile ran parallel to the road in a quiet darkness. Good hiding place for a body.

The knife flashed. There was a pause; the kind of pause that defies time. It was a sharp pull inwards to a silence that even a knife could not cut, for it was more permanent than this body; a separate construction completely which he had never entered though now it seemed so familiar. And from it, Steven heard his mouth echo forcefully into the musky air of the taxi, "Let... me... out... of...

this... car!" And then again, "Let... me... out... of... this... car!"

It had the clarity of an elocution practice, of the type that his temperament had buckled under at school - he had always sat at the back when poetry was looming and had got away with it because there was something beautiful about him that no one wanted to see ridiculed.

"Let... me... out... now!" A third time.

The man stretched in front of him.

'Now he's going to do it,' Steven imagined, as the taxi driver's arm stretched towards him. The moment was lightning quick, but his thoughts were a slow commentary by some perfectly safe aspect of himself that was merely observing.

But the arm stretched over him. He felt its heavy heat on his chest. It lifted the metal handle and the door opened. The man said nothing and Steven simply got out. He saw the lights dancing on the water. From some obscure memory he felt the benign presence of a father standing next to him saying, 'Look at the junks, Steven.'

The taxi was gone. He was on his own standing in the dark. He could not feel his body, but his hand went to the purse. He was not dead and the purse was still there.

What now? He walked a few yards on legs he still could not feel. Then he walked back. Stood. An immense calmness, deeper than the numbness of shock, made him able to do nothing, just wait. It would be all right.

A car pulled up. Its lights were bright, unreal almost. Steven had heard it swerve round as though the driver had been told to turn and stop and help. How could he have seen Steven on the side of the road?

A head looked out of the window. It spoke English.

"Are you lost?"

"Yes, I'm looking for a youth hostel. It's over the other side of the bridge."

"You're miles away. Get in. We'll take you."

Steven got in not stopping to think. He would keep quiet about the taxi. Children squashed against him in the back. They had been to a party and smelt of food. The wife was in the front. No one spoke much. It was as if a task was to be done, nothing more. But with more than relief, Steven impulsively loved the whole family, however many of them there were; loved them like people one has not seen for half a century, but had once been at home with.

They drew up outside the hostel gates. Someone was locking up. It was now one-thirty. Steven leapt out. Thanked them very, very much, but they hurried him as anxious as he for his safety. He noticed as the man looked out of the window again that he was Indian.

The tee-shirted gatekeeper shrugged when Steven asked him why he was locking up so late. He did not understand English and it did not matter anyway.

Steven lay in the narrow bed in the dark thinking. It was not so much the shock of the event that kept him alert as the sense of not being alone. There were five other people asleep in the room, but they were just the quietly heaving bodies of other student travellers; anonymous lumps in the darkness. Fleetingly he realised that had it been Patrick or Pete lying there he would have felt the same.

The presence in the room had begun to convey itself with the gatekeeper's opening up of the hostel, the swerving of the car, the Indian mother's warmth. It was a truth with which danger - and the distant release of his mother's hand - had put him in touch. And was so distinctly here, in this shabby youth hostel bedroom, that to sleep would have been an impertinence.

But he was tired and the mind can only extend so far in its response to what it cannot perceive sensually. In the end it has to turn back to a familiar route; which is why people breaking new ground spiritually can get so tired. They push and push and lacking the patience required to take the last few steps - those slow, slippery, last steps - they revert back, not having learned stillness, to the familiarity of what they have tried so hard to be free from. Unsurprising then that Steven's sleep was long and heavy. When he woke the room was empty. The other students, travellers with their bodies only, had left.

He sat up in the silence and listened to it. It met him from last night, so pronounced that he could not disturb it; not even with the calm swing of his body out of bed. It was making a claim on him as clear as a person addressing him. So he just lay waiting, easily able in the aftermath of sleep to be passive.

Sun poured through the dusty windows. It was going to be hot. This added to the stillness and to the relaxation of his body so that it hardly seemed to exist. And without it all the concerns that constituted his life fell away. It was not important whether they went to Luxor or not; whether he flew home next week or the week after.

The waves his mind were making were from a different, bigger sea than that.

At university Steven read on average four books a week on top of his routine work. Often he made notes in a small black book he had set aside for his personal learning. He enjoyed watching the extra novels and biographies add up. He seemed to be growing, becoming more rounded and authoritative.

One such novel lay on his pillow. He had intended to read a few pages before sleeping but shock had made it irrelevant. And now the silence, gathering force and depth, holding him inside it as in an invisible room - quite disparate from this poky, Egyptian one - the silence made the book look inferior.

It was in fact an excellent book; had been recommended by his tutor. But from here, along with his rucksack, his canvas shoes, his jeans hanging off the end of his bed like legs about to leap, it seemed part of another world.

When Patrick, Pete and he stood in front of the only coloured carving at the Karnatak temple two days later, swigging fizzy water and wiping sweat from their faces, Steven felt the silence again. This time it was a knife cutting the connection between him and his friends. He did not hear them laughing and joking; was alone in a stillness which was both exciting and frightening. It was as though someone had opened a trap door and he was falling through himself, down, down to a point of stillness that no one could reach.

Afterwards as they walked out of the temple, Steven was jolly in a way that did not match the heat of the long day behind them. He agreed for the first time to join Patrick and Pete at a night club. But in bed at three, he lay awake feeling guilty like a child who has spent his money the wrong way.

The next term at university Steven wrote seven essays. Each one was a careful compilation of critics' comments about a different author - Durack, Joyce, Shakespeare. And each was also a gift of homage to Williamson, his tutor, whom he admired for his book-lined room, the flick of his grey hair, his wry humour and even, masochistically for the fact that his essays were always given 'B' and so kept the man on a pedestal.

It was the ninth week of term. Steven had flu and had only managed notes not an essay. He walked along the tree-lined path to the English block, drained and determined. Just as he was turning into the grounds, that silence which he had forgotten (for silence is as hard as pain to recall) filled him again. This time it came as a gentleness, like an arm round his shoulder. It contrasted so much with the anxiously written sheaf of notes under his arm that he nearly threw them in the litter bin he was passing. But he pulled himself together and interpreted this sudden serenity as a sign that he should persevere with his studies.

His confidence won Williamson's confidence. Skimming through the notes, he told Steven that if he had written them up he would have achieved his first alpha. Then pushing them back across his desk, he began to talk of his own work: research for a book on fourteenth century mysticism. Steven took his comments as a compliment, not realising that the man was merely spilling over, enjoying an audience.

How could Steven, flattered, excited, ambitious, have known at that point that silence, not Williamson, was his teacher? For silence is humble; will shape itself to the most twisted and troubled of minds, like a river finding its way over rocks until it reaches the ocean, leaving a person free to stumble undisturbed towards their own intelligence while Williamson's intelligence urged and pushed one conspicuously towards itself so that conversation with him was an unhappy gorging on his words in the absence of one's own. Steven was becoming fat on Williamson's attentions but inside he was a starved child.

Nonetheless, for the next two terms leading up to finals, he worked incredibly hard; set a routine to which he stuck with an extremism that was deep in his nature. It seemed to be the right thing for a promising student to do. Between family commitments and chapters on mysticism, Williamson encouraged him. The starved child - watching his erudition grow like a great rock forming out of grains: tiny, spidery notes in spiral pads - did nothing to dissuade him; waited at his door, simply.

At night it gained confidence; wandered freely through his dreams; woke him up sometimes, made him jump out of bed to jot down an idea. But in the morning the idea looked ridiculous. Steven physically blushed in the empty room at its naïveté and would hurry to the words of a published critic to reconfirm his adulthood.

But the child was powerful. It kept him awake more and more. Steven began to find himself in two worlds: a night world and a day world. When he came to finals, he was in a twilight that won him a middle second. Middle means Muddle. He was devastated. It was worse than a third. Beautiful people got thirds.

But his spirit was on the road...

GOD

*Master of space,
the cedar is broad enough
to see all viewpoints
but his lateral aim
is to concede nothing.*

Steven began to find himself in two worlds: a night world and a day world...

The silence is three days old. It gives the room a clean feeling. For three days no one has stood and thought, 'I'll have a cup of tea now' or, 'Damn these shoes, it's time for some new ones.' No one has touched the cushions, snuggled into the chairs, put their hand on the table and felt the cold shine of wood on their palm as they mention the broken drain. No one has sat with their feet on the tightly upholstered footstool with the phone to their ear, listening and nodding and pointing with their spare hand to the kitchen where the oven needs to be switched off or the fruit cake will be burned. No one has changed the cold autumn air with the two red bars of heat or changed the bright overhead light for lamplight.

Only the smell of them lingers; the smell that suggests that older people live here. They are not as rich as they used to be; choose the cheap soup in the supermarket and yet have a nineteenth century porcelain pot to keep paper clips in and anything else - "Do you want this old tie pin, Andrew?"

"No, not really..."

"I'll pop it in the pot then shall I?"

It is a smell of pipe and cat and the fruit bowls of still lives. And Steven, tired from the city, rests in it as he stands in the doorway. He has come for the week-end.

"That will be marvellous, Steven. Are you sure you don't mind being on your own?" (Steven, twenty-five, unmarried.)

"No, fine, no problem. It'll be a break."

Steven sits for a few moments on the floral sofa, his suitcase still in the doorway. This indefinable silence is a sweetness that is so familiar. It is also the result of his body relaxing, having been for a week at the beck and call of other people's thoughts: 'wish he'd do this... wish he'd ring... wish he wouldn't stand like that... put his hand through his hair like that.'

People like Steven. He is a part of their thinking enough to make an unidentifiable stress in his body. He sometimes feels this current prompting him to get up quickly to the next matter that is calling. And the matter is only a shirt to iron, but the shirt is somehow alive and demanding because muddled with it is so-and-so's thought about his being rather strident today. So he hurries on with the cuffs as though his life depended on them.

And now he is alone and quiet with no one to talk to him but his mother who has written a note: 'Darling, lots of yoghurt and cheese in the fridge and extra bread in the freezer. See you on Sun.' The quietness is pleasant but it is tinged with the forlornness that comes of being in a place one has outgrown.

He goes up to his room, preoccupied with his morning's meeting. He had to explain his design for a book cover. It was a good idea. He knew it; knew, as it had formed itself in the Sydney traffic, that it was more than just an attractive design. Sure, it needed the organised hand of a draughtsman to make it work, but the idea was definitely powerful. Steven understands the feel of ideas; knows they are either there or they are not. He had been confident. Most of his ideas had been accepted and his reputation was good.

'Why did they reject it? Look, if a book is about a voyage and the voyage is a metaphor for an exploration into the psyche, you do not just have a picture of tangled nets in the sunlight against the sea with a man yellow-jacketed and sunburnt stretching across the deck. You have something allegorical: you have an authentic photo of the ship merging into the cloud so that it seems unreal, don't you?'

Yes. Maybe one does. But if it is time for someone to change, no matter how good an idea, fate will take a hand and a decision will deflect. In this case, Paul Hart had a headache and Steven's brown suit annoyed him. Rejection flared in him and he tore the design to bits. His wife had been wearing a brown suit when she had handed him her lawyer's letter requesting divorce proceedings. So Steven's idea was rejected because the mild approval of the rest of the committee was not powerful enough to oppose Paul Hart's unhappiness.

Steven had left the boardroom carrying his portfolio. 'Calm down. What's one failure?' Month after month he had left that same room with instructions to go ahead: 'Yes, fine, go for it! Contact David, get it into the pipeline.' Did it matter this once? He had not been given the sack. They would all forget it by the end of the day, get into their cars and drive home for the week-end.

But Steven is intense about work. There are a hundred rooms in his house - on the walls are imprinted images far more vivid than this single one - but he lives only in one room: his office, for that is defined by someone else and is therefore easy. And now even that room is shut so his mind does not know where to go.

He draws the curtains, gets out a novel from his overnight bag and sits in the chair by the window. His mother had upholstered this chair ten or so summers ago. He remembers her kneeling on their old conservatory floor swearing at the blunt needle, surrounded by scraps of kapok, the sun warming her then brown hair. It was her first attempt at upholstery and her ineptitude can still be felt in the lumps under Steven's leg. But the chair takes him back to a full time; a time when there was sea and soft breezes, when he woke to the sound of gulls landing on the porch roof. The sun had always shone in that garden; that big garden with its welcoming smell of honeysuckle. It had been a little heaven enclosed by ancient walls with its creepers, its creaking swing, sprawling bushes of mint, hydrangeas so large he could wash his face in them, an orchard gate that had to be kept closed or the sheep would chew the vegetables. Rising early and running down and out into the warm mist before breakfast knowing it was going to be really hot, taking off his knitted royal blue jumper; and the sound of his father putting out the milk bottles on the porch, and then a snatch of tawny brown as the slim figure of the man disappeared up the front stairs to shave and look out onto his garden with white foam on his chin. That blessed time, he enters, and warms himself on it.

That man with whom he had shared nature, who had taught him how to fish, how to balance the float on the brown river; who had shown him how dogs sit to a whistle and how to shoot clay pigeons, that man is dead. And now there is Andrew, stripy-shirted and electric: toaster, shaver, blender, mower, calculator. A man who does not have string in a pocket but a plastic bubble of shining clips on a card in a drawer; who has a slim black case with papers in it which he sits on his lap after dinner, where his real father had an old leather box with gold plated initials for his pipe. He wrote very slowly with the odd capital letter in the middle of the word, but beautifully as though to the queen, where Andrew's is the scrawl of the doctor he is not. The comparison breaks the warmth and his mind jolts out of the honeysuckle garden back into this yellow room.

And inside the yellow room the feel of the radiator is cold and hard on his numbing hand. It is as if by going into the past he has forgotten to give breath and blood to his body and now it pulls him. So here he is. But what is here? He travels the drawers and cupboards of the house trying to find a resonance: the sixties suits under plastic covers, the off-cuts of old wallpaper at the back of shelves, the book case with its Neville Shutes and Rosemary Sutcliffes; Book Society choices for Jenny who likes someone to do the choosing for her - prefers the good sense of a man (suited, cultured).

Steven knows every corner of the house because he had helped them move in, using up his holiday out of some old guilt that he had not supported his mother and wanted to see her settled. He had worked tee-shirted and hot in the December sun carrying tables and chairs and sitting for twenty minutes with the workmen on the wall to drink a coke, feeling rather closer to them than he did to his mother and this man she had married; which often happens these days, that his affinities go to strangers in tiny exchanges that have no complications.

It makes him a stranger to the house and his mind veers back to work. He walks around his office, sits on the swivel chair in front of the in-tray and the china pig full of pens, looks into the soft green of the mountain trees in the picture on his desk which is his comfort when the strip lighting buzzes and made-up women with brass-buttoned little jackets make him feel jaded and choked. He pictures his friend Sam; tall, kind, understanding, loafing in the doorway saying, 'Come on Steve, let's go for coffee,' and their talks in the canteen when Steven confesses, 'Sam, I'm just not interested in women right now. I don't know why... maybe they just take up too much space...' There is affection between them because Sam is in a different phase from Steven and his distance makes him an easy confidant. But mixed up with Sam is the office and the office has just said 'no' to him; has done what he had always dreaded it might:

rejected his imagination. And the dread is born of the knowledge that success can go from one in a second; that even talent is an unsteady foundation upon which to build a palace. But where is there firmer ground?

It is getting late, and accumulated tension makes his mind tumble and rush to all kinds of people and places. It is a tension which sex might relieve but Steven has no one. So the tension turns back on itself and becomes apathy. He undresses, throws his clothes on the chair - if his design had been accepted he would have folded them - and sleeps.

It is early when Steven wakes. He is calm now, happy almost, for it is Saturday and - design or no design - he can do as he pleases. Failure has made his future a blur. Often he brings work down here to Kempsie but there is not much he can get on with until he receives the go-ahead from Paul Hart who is the start and finishing line of his life.

He dresses and goes down to the kitchen, eats a bowl of cereal standing up and listens to the news without hearing it. At ten the phone rings. It is Sunita, his step-sister. She is surprised to hear his voice; was not expecting him to be there, thought she might pop down to see Dad for the weekend.

"Didn't you know? Your Dad and Mum have gone to the Gold Coast. I'm looking after the place."

"Oh. I've been travelling around a bit lately. Never mind. Anyway, how are things with you?"

"Fine," he replies. She hears his despondency. They do not know each other well, were young adults when their parents married and have not a lot in common. She is a nurse at Sydney's Westmede Hospital.

"You're welcome to come down anyway," he finds himself saying, "if you want to get out of the city."

She pauses with the hesitation of someone whose personality is essentially easygoing but who has imposed certain conditions upon it.

"Can we leave it open?" she asks. He agrees and, self-absorbed, soon forgets her and goes to the shop to buy a jar of coffee. He wanders around the rose gardens on his way back.

At twelve she is standing on the doorstep waiting.

"I've got a key but didn't have it with me," she says, smiling as he comes through the gate.

It is odd to think that this house is as much hers as his even though neither of them grew up here. She is a stranger to him, but he thinks, watching her put her bag on the work top, that she is prettier than he remembered. Her face is soft. 'She must be going out with some guy,' he thinks. It is nice that they are brother and sister; it takes the edge off their meeting while there is still the interest that comes of knowing each other so little.

Saturday stretches before him with more promise than it had earlier. Sunita suggests a walk, "Or have you just come back from one?" Then hurries on with, "Why not a picnic? I'm so sick of being inside smelly hospitals." She laughs. Clearly it does not matter to her that her work is tedious.

"The ward I'm working on is full of bed-wetting geriatrics. One had his foot amputated yesterday." She imitates the old man's last farewell to his hideous toes; relates how she had been hard put to control her laughter when he had addressed them as old friends one at a time: "Good-bye, Big Toe." She giggles. He can tell she is a good nurse. Her body is efficient and strong but she is able to laugh. He likes her for that because he doesn't laugh enough.

"Okay," he agrees, "a picnic then."

They look in the larder for biscuits and bread, foraging amongst the pots of jam. For a moment Steven is embarrassed that it is his mother who has made jam and that she is married to Sunita's father. Sunita feels his awkwardness and says something nice about home-made jam, how she would never bother: "all that stirring and stuff." And they come out into the kitchen carrying only a bar of cooking chocolate, she laughing again.

She changes into jeans and one of her father's jumpers which she takes from his bedroom cupboard. It comes down to her knees almost but she feels happy in it because it is a relief after a week in bri-nylon and elasticated belts. Steven wants to hug her, but she goes to the door.

They walk to the river, he carrying the basket ahead of her. The grass is still wet from the night rain and it soaks through his shoes coldly though the sun is now really bright. Then he slips, sliding onto his bottom like a child. She laughs and puts her hand out to help him. He feels at once stupid and touched: her hand a steadying influence he remembers from somewhere else. Her laughter blocks out the memory. They continue walking, in silence now, and he feels Friday falling away.

The river is a brown snake of water winding down from the hills. Eventually it joins Sydney Harbour, but they catch it where it is narrow. Andrew had wanted to buy a house by the sea but Jenny had persuaded him not to, wanting a quiet place. And their differences repeat gently in Steven and Sunita - she sun, he rain; she people, he quiet - as they stand now by the water.

She picks up a stone, skims it across the sparkling water. It jumps four times, and the heron resting on a rock lifts its stick legs and flies off. She tells him how much she loves it here and often comes to visit. He watches her body as it bends to pick up a colourful pebble and feels its harmony. She doesn't seem to care if he is there or not.

She walks beside him showing him things: a leaf-coloured cavern in the cliff face, wooden stumps in the mud which she says are the remains of an old rowing boat. And he wonders out loud at how little he has noticed about this place before.

"That's because you don't look. You're too inward," she claims. He doesn't mind her saying it. It is as free of nastiness as her laughter about old man's toes. They are eating cooking chocolate.

Other people have tried this before. A group of students once, caring but inept, confronted him with, 'You're in your own world, Steve.' And he had kicked them out for their entry was forceful. With her softness he says nothing.

"Look!" She squints up river. "I reckon it's Lucy and Nick." Friends of their parents. She stands up and waves, her cheerful greeting as important it seems as her gentle walk through his mind. He realises what is so special about her is this odd way in which her kindness has no preferences; and she interacts well with life.

She turns to him. Again the ease is the greater for them being nominally brother and sister. It makes her unafraid and him relaxed. Her face is close to his. She sees in him a quality so precious she wants to cup his chin, to point to it as she has to the cavern and the old boat. She sees it so clearly as she had not five years ago when they had drunk to the continued happiness of their parents. He had seemed to her sallow then and she to him too bouncy. But neither had been comfortable on that occasion and so what were actually their strengths had made them seem unnatural.

"Steve," (Her hair is falling out of its pony tail. Her skin is pale. It does not matter) "Steve, I think you're very special." Innocence makes her unsentimental, but he raises an eyebrow and sniggers nervously.

A dinghy sails past. He tells her about the book cover and how he's fed up with Paul Hart. She gets him to relate the whole story: the office, the people, Sam. She is a good listener; nods; occasionally drifting off as a bird lands or the sun makes designs through the cloud. But he likes that too. It is like talking to himself which he has always wanted to do but won't in case anyone sees him silently moving his lips or, more to the point, in case it really is the first sign of madness.

He concludes: "So that's it. I'll probably get the sack."

She laughs.

"Course you won't. I gave a guy the wrong antibiotics once and he came out in great lumps. That's much worse." He agrees but cannot find the words to tell her it is something deeper than that he is fearing. She knows.

"Look," she says, a little more serious, for they have reached a point of intensity for her too. "Steve," (she is beautiful now not pretty) "it doesn't matter. It really doesn't matter." Her softness has gone.

"Maybe it's because I work with people who have nothing. I mean, some of these old biddies have nothing. They can't talk some of them." She imitates their gobbledygook and they laugh. "I promise you it doesn't matter." She is looking at his awkward body. "Look, you'll never be a Paul Hart however hard you try." This both hurts and exhilarates him. "You just won't, and you'll always fall short if that's what you're aiming for. It's people that matter anyway. It's feelings not a smooth output. You know, if you ever tried talking with God it might put things in perspective a bit." She says it shyly, hating evangelism and reluctant to admit to the source of her certainty but forced to it, for rescuing him is more important than saving her own face. And it works to God's advantage. Her diffidence touches him as stridency would not have done. The tenderness in her admission makes it real.

"You're very special. That's obvious the moment one sees you," she continues, forgetting the impression she had first had of him. "You don't need to make a big deal of it. If *you're* pleased with your allegorical ship, that's all that matters. Look Steve," (her stridency is because she is relaxed) "neither of us can be confined to that limited world." She cannot find the words to make it sound attractive. She only has the language of tendons and ligaments so she says it as it is: "We are treading the same path."

He makes his world seem small. She is holding it in her hand and laughing at it and he wants to join her, but it has been important to him for too long.

"Why did Andrew call you Sunita?" he asks, trying to disarm her.

"His first girlfriend was Indian, I think," she answers only to get it out of the way. Again he is reminded of something and again she cuts across the grasping of his memory and goes on with her destruction, frighteningly knowledgeable about the world he works in.

"How do you know it's like that?" Petulant now, a small boy on the defensive.

"Because, Steve, the whole world's like that." And now the whole world is on her hand and she dissects it in two swift cuts: "Too much impressing. Too much compromise."

"How old are you?" He tries to disarm her again; a masculine trick he is not masterful in.

"Twenty-two." It excuses her being so absolute while bringing to it a poignancy. For here is a young person's view of a world that had been handed down to her with so much affection. Andrew had taken her out to dinner several times and tried to help shape her future. She had been open because she loved the man but cool because she did not love his world.

She stops.

"Hey Steve, what's the time?" She puts her hand to her mouth like the child she is not. "I'm on call from eight. Shit, I forgot."

"I thought you were staying the night." It is an innocent question.

"I was, but I forgot."

Racing back she is all muddle and rush. She runs upstairs, pulls off the jumper and stuffs it back in her father's drawer. Steven wants to brush her hair, straighten her shirt, touch her, but she runs to the door. Her face is bright with panic but also with intensity. It does not matter that she leaves now for they have recognised each other.

He sits on the floral sofa again. It feels less forlorn now that Sunita has blown in and out. Somehow she has stirred up the atmosphere so that the silence here has a lighter, happier quality. He remembers her words: 'talking with God... might put things in perspective a bit.' Why did she say 'talk with' and not pray, he wondered? Anyway he had done neither since his father had died.

Besides there is an anger in him that he suffered this loss so young. It made him treat Andrew badly. But about praying, it's just for wallies, isn't it? Sunita is no wally. She is lovely. And innocent. A part of him is desperate, he realises. 'Oh God, I feel stupid. There, I've already started. I've said, Oh God.' His mind wanders to the edge of the Nile. He remembers the paternal presence he had felt. And immediately the same silence floods his mind. He spoils it with an image of Williamson leaning back in his chair, but the silence overpowers him; makes cynicism look small-minded. He is in that delicious quietness again that is like a rest from all effort; a return to comfort that makes the whole of his life look like the struggle of a fish out of water. He feels a sense of belonging in the silence and starts to recall the other times he experienced it, wondering how he could have forgotten. Of course, the Indian mother in the car... is that who Sunita reminded him of, or was there something else...? The rest is now not just a freedom from hassle, from his own body, it is a new room to live in.

"God?" he questions. The embarrassment is gone. The silence intensifies. He feels himself cushioned in a warm glow as if he is on cool fire. 'God!' The single word is all he can manage. Tears stream down his cheeks that have not felt the sting of salt since someone kicked a football in his face at school. A great pain is going from him.

On Monday morning Steven takes the bus to the office. Leaning against the window he feels so calm that he does not even wonder what will happen today. He is governed by a new force which makes success and failure feel the same.

"Steve, guess what?" Sam meets him at the door and catches his arm. "Guess what? The cover's going through."

"What?" alive with feeling.

"Paul decided over the week-end. Said he'd gone for a walk on Saturday afternoon and thought it over. Could see your point, tried to ring you, but you were out."

"I went for a walk too."

"Great, eh?"

"Yeah. Yeah, fantastic."

They go together to the lift, their thoughts moving easily in mutual understanding, for they had been friends at university; had known each other in another freer context than this.

"Guess what too, Steve? Rachel and I got engaged."

"Engaged! Great!" They are on the fourth floor, strolling through the open plan office. He turns to face Sam and puts his hands on his shoulders.

"Fantastic!" Sincere because he compares the news with his own week-end.

"Steve..." Paul comes out from his office, smiling and using words he usually sneers at: "I expect Sam told you. I had a change of heart." And there they are, all carried in the same upward swing.

The office hums. Sylvia walks past sloshing coffee, giggles and swears as she puts it down on the desk she shares with Chrissy. She slams open and closed a couple of drawers looking for Tippex that is not clogged. A hundred telephones ring. Mike sits on the edge of his desk, casual, yet his voice insistent. Someone else is writing noiselessly but his mind is electric and maddened by an unreasonable deadline. And everyone is caffeinated, breathing fast and shallow. But for this little circle of peace where the three men stand by the window.

Paul Hart strolls back into his office, looks at the photo of his wife and children that might now have been twisting and turning in the refuse lorry clanking along the street below. Sam tidies his desk, not quite ready for serious work and then sits back, tilting his chair, thinking, 'Soon I'll have a photo of Rachel in a silver frame, just there,' touching the space in front of him on his desk, 'and it will be of her standing on a Cretan beach.' He tilts his chair a little too far and it topples and everyone's laughter is around him as it had been in his school days when he had ragged the teachers with mischievous charm. And they all think, 'Nice guy.'

And Steven stays by the window and watches his colleagues. He sees them as ordinary people now, not walking intellects. Then he goes to the phone and rings Sunita - she had scribbled her number on her stepmother's shopping list - to thank her and tell her she is right about the office, that it's all silly and, 'anyway, they accepted my design after all, for what it's worth.' There is a silence as she pulls him back from an extreme that is as dangerous as his desire to please.

"Steve," (gently) "it's not silly. It's just not everything."

He is exasperated for he likes things complete and she is unfolding in front of him a path with no end, a balance never found. He has always moved along so fast, sprinted to the point of self-destruction;

pulled himself away from the crowd; or else moseyed along, a flaccid indistinct part of it.

"Sunita, er, what you said about God. Can we talk about it?"

"Yeah, sure." She is cool, but behind her coolness is the same fire. In the conversation she is solid, careful, involved, funny, but as easily and quickly alone and concentrated like a runner concerned for a friend but aware of the track before her from which she cannot afford to be distracted.

"Then we'll meet next week, okay?" she says, calming his urgency; conscious, for this stretch of the path at least, they will walk together.

He puts the phone down, surprised that he is not disappointed by her coolness and is aware that it is arbitrary little kindnesses that make life great, not strings of achievements. Jenny flashes into his head, and he feels how much ground he has to make up there. Poor Mum.

The rest of the day passes in a slow quietness. He gets through his work and by the afternoon he has forgotten all else. But her calmness and the silence is in the steady line of his pen.

ANGEL

Struck dumb by lightning.
out of this disaster
rose a sad majesty
of the mountain ash.

He realises what is so special about her is this odd way in which her kindness has no preferences; and she interacts well with life...

An angel is the best of what a person has always been: the honesty that makes it hard to tell a lie or the courage that makes superficiality so loathsome. It is the part of a person that can be overlaid but not changed.

Physically it is as a body, but its features will be those that have characterised many faces. Repeated qualities form the face of an angel. For matter changes by circumstance in texture and form not in essence.

This angel has been mother, father, child; has sat at the heart of gatherings; has stood alone by dark water and wished only for solitude; has tried to change people, has preached vehemently against it; has filled its orbit with people and as strongly pushed them away; has spoken many languages and adopted many customs with the ease of one whose culture rises above them all. The angel is a still balance of all its own impulses; a being resolved rather than compromised.

And being resolved, the fluctuations of circumstance still themselves around him. People slow down and reassess in his presence; are able on the plainness of his mind to project their pain, look at it and find in it a blessing.

He works in the space between past and future; in the infinitesimal units that make up the present. Love has stripped him of all but an essence that comes into form only when a task is to be done. Otherwise he is silent.

His talent, once an intricate, many-roomed building, has been sold and divided for those with nowhere else to live. Once, he directed the use of his assets. Now he is simply the wisdom in someone else's manipulation of wealth.

He hangs as a crystal between people and possessions, people and each other, people and nature, returning each to themselves so that at the time of separation they can part without pain.

He has a quiet ruthlessness born of his experience of the past, his knowledge of the future and because he is preparing to house an entity so subtle that only the peace of bare walls can accommodate it. And yet, living in the present, he hurries no one; neither urges solitude, nor intimacy, but illuminates whatever is happening so that ordinary actions done in his presence become special.

All of which he has learned from God whom he has kept parallel to himself as a lover keeps parallel his partner; has her there watching, invisibly judging each action, each thought - 'would she like this?' And God is a wisdom which signals the angel to use his senses more deeply: see beyond, hear behind...

Before, he had often wanted to tell someone, to test his truth on the sensible mind of a friend. But always some circumstance stood in the way. And if not circumstance, then memory would fail him so that, sitting in a wrought iron chair drinking tea in the sun with a person he trusted, he would forget what he had wanted to say. It belonged to another world to which tea-time ordinariness had no access.

And when his life became a single secret embodied, that made everything external an irrelevance, it burst out into this new form: which is Angel.

We meet him now in the quiet atmosphere of a Swiss sitting room where Mori, a German composer, is reading a book. Angel is not visible nor felt at this point, but his mind is pulled here, responding to the task with the same intensity that he might once have shown to a woman. And yet once the work is done he will simply withdraw.

Mori has come to Switzerland for a break. His wife has died. She was his strength and vitality. His music was his own but its movement from page to hands, from hands to public ears, was hers. She moved his talent for him, while his own motivation lay dormant. He felt guilty about that. And so when one Sunday morning she lay in bed very ill, the essence of him allowed her death. She had grown ill from giving and her fifty-year-old body could take no more. Mori's devastation was such that he could not stay in the city, nor in the country, for people spoke of her - she was like Mahler's Alma - and he could not bear it.

Switzerland's white quietness reflects his need to be clean of her. It is hard. He is angry and he takes his anger out on shopkeepers, taxi drivers, people in the street, for they cannot proliferate it. He can walk away from them, their reactions hitting the air in untargeted abuse. It is hard strolling back into the chalet, cheese in a bag under one arm, newspaper rolled under the other, to meet the silence. Erike had been omnipresent in their Bonn house; in the cushions, the sagging sofa, the pictures, the paperbacks left half-read face down on the rosewood table, in the broken chopping board in the kitchen, the smiley badge on the fridge and most of all in the air of the place. The smell of her perfume was in the curtains, the carpet, the rugs, so that coming in to compose he met her invisibly and his music came as a greeting. Here in this rented chalet there is no Erike.

But there is Angel, whose world is of such a different order that the mind in matter can barely grasp it. In quiet times the imagination can come within glimpsing distance of it; for imagination can find in itself a lightness uneclipsed by sorrow. Angel is waiting for Mori to find this thread-thin light.

And the glimpse will expand into a vision and Mori will see a place where communication is condensed into a single thought, a look, a movement. Its medium is imagery which is also why the imagination is sensitive to it.

Angel is a creator of images which as quickly as they are formed are sent like letters; personal letters that speak to a heart whose breaking is an advantage for it makes paths along which his messages can travel.

So what will he do today? Swim? He has discipline (which she had not; was easily bored), has planned daily exercise to keep his grieving body strong; will stay through the winter to ski away feeling. For some reason he forbids himself to ring friends, several of whom are in Lucerne following the music festival. He has a row of books to read and occasionally stretching his concentration to a full page has found a phrase or two that please him. But on the whole the books seem poor.

He will walk then. Today he will just walk, for the fresh air helps. He tries to convince himself as he puts the single plate and mug in the sink, that it is good for him not to be working for a couple of months. He cannot go on and on creating; not without her. He has to adjust to patches of ordinariness. More, his essentially optimistic mind looks for blessings in the pain. Maybe he will eventually write some good music out of all this.

He puts on his topsider shoes, the ones he had worn sailing in France two summers ago. He puts on his jacket, the one he used to wear on summer Saturday mornings when they shopped. He goes out to the top of the sloping drive, then changes his mind. He returns, fetches francs from the wooden drawer of the cheap sideboard, bundles them into his pocket and walks towards the town.

Angel watches; is simply there. As such, he is the brother of trees and plants, for he does not plan. His mind is plain.

Mori walks into a small expensive clothes store. He must have new trousers and shirt. He cannot wait. A friendly assistant helps him and he allows her to select blue checks and beige corduroy, for in his grief he has lost the clarity of preference. It is as he was when a boy, his mother choosing, putting her head round the changing room curtain to look and he letting her straighten collar, sigh at the trouser hem.

He takes the garments and goes to buy shoes. Here he knows what he wants. Suede lace-ups. The assistant, again helpful, eases on the shoe. He wishes he could sit back on the chair and shut his eyes, but she is telling him they fit fine, Monsieur, and he has to get up to pay.

He returns to Chalet d'Ogez and enters the small bedroom whose view is a solid bank of flowers. He changes into his new clothes. He will walk this afternoon instead. More coffee. The patio. His book.

He nestles in his new clothes in the sun and relaxes. The book is boring. He closes his eyes against the blue sky for its blankness glares onto his blank spirit.

And now he is lovely to Angel. His body calmed by fresh clothes, his mind lulled by sunlight, his blankness is good, for it provides a safe landing; a solid grey airstrip for the angel's similarly calm mind.

Angel's work is delicate. He is a plane landing on a moving, heaving runway or a creature alighting on a leaf that may transform into a hungry, camouflaged animal. He has no choice but to go there, for a task is to be done; a soul saved. He goes to Mori with no intention to pry or to take. His mind has its qualities and experiences merged in a wash of colour which if decorated by another's would lose its own beauty.

The movement of these beings is as a light shadow of our movement here. They walk as we do, smile as we do, but their ears are accustomed only to silence. So that coming into matter is like entering a vast and screaming piece of machinery; breath like the windswept suck and hiss of the sea, touch like the fall of a mountain on one's head. It is a shock.

Angel foresees the shock; knows that soon he will re-enter that loudness which was once his everyday environment and for this short, blessed time has simply been a place to visit; the context of his work.

Mori opens his eyes and looks at the sky, able to face its azure brightness more easily, for sleep has soothed him. Angel is seated beside him as still and unneeding of acknowledgement as the tree on the slope outside.

Mori puts the book down which is filled, like his topsiders and jacket, with someone else's life and struggle. He dozes again, this time peacefully. His eyes feel like they are sinking into his head, his face losing its features, smoothed and blanketed into warm comfortableness.

There is a talent in there. It hides in his personality like jade in a rock, indistinguishable except in the rise and fall of his music. It illuminates him sometimes - which was why Erike had been attracted. She noticed his face and loved it, for recognition comes more clearly before speech begins. But the recognition was brief and soon it was his music that she loved. And then her attention went to his name and reputation.

And now Angel's mind is drawn to the ordinariness that Erike's departure has led to. It can relax in the open space that a sudden kiss, the sound of her voice from the study, the twist of her silk dressing-gowned figure had made. Even ten years after their marriage (for both their second) Mori's sensitive body and mind had moved to her sound.

And passing across him soundlessly, Angel need not hurry in as an intruder, but can move slowly and easily, for it is a merged place in Mori he seeks: the money under the mattress, the treasure in the outhouse; the essence of the man. And he passes through the rooms seeing what Mori has gathered: feelings, fears, actions, patterns of notes that resound again and again; the partying wit, the sadness, the attraction to blue before red, chocolate before cheese. And these he does not touch. But the brightness in his being, of which Mori is unaware - for life has not yet pushed him to it - he chips at over a space of weeks, like a carver.

And because Mori is suffering he does not notice Angel at work. When pain rises through his body in a wave as he sits to write a letter; when he wakes to warm sun on his face, he connects it with his wife and pushes himself into the next scene, manipulating his body only by a massive act of will. Feet which had once danced for hours drag as they do after too long swimming.

And in the numbness that follows, Angel works as a dentist works to clean a cavity before filling it: scrapes, drills, washes. For what is to take the place of all this congestion of feeling is an innocence that needs space and light to emerge into. And he works with the care of someone who has himself been drilled. He knows when to pressurise and when to lay off; so that one evening Mori succumbs to a hospitality he has hitherto felt to be wrong, and enjoys a wine and cheese party. His friends remark on his cheerfulness, but it is only an interlude.

Mori learns to live with pain as a man with a wife he has stopped loving; acknowledges it on waking, gives it place in his planning: 'Can't go swimming, might meet Michelle; she'll remind me of...' And he settles it before sleep in a dreary monologue, 'Come on Mori, you'll get through it.'

And when in February he returns to Bonn, he is stronger; has built a compartment for his sadness where before it permeated his whole being. He is still not looking forward to walking into the house, but he must, for there are papers to sort, bills to pay. He had left so abruptly he had forgotten to ask Frau Klein to come in and clean. The place smells. Not of perfume.

He is energetic. Phones the woman to come immediately. She cannot refuse because she feels sorry for him. And he sits in the mess of the drawing room, as she cleans around him, and sorts out the bills. No one knows he is back, so it is quiet, but for snatches of Frau Klein's song as she vacuums the stairs. He doesn't mind. He makes coffee for them both. The smiley badge on the fridge makes his heart lurch, but he pushes the beat back into rhythm and throws the thing into the bin.

She chatters about her family; her son who has just wrecked his car, her daughter who has just found a new boyfriend. Finding her tactlessness comforting, he opens his letters.

Letters mean life. People. Plans. His head starts ringing and the phone rings with it.

"Mori, I just thought of you. How are you? Could you come for dinner...? Next week? Fine... The Akademie's looking forward to having you back... A couple of meetings coming up... Okay, see you then."

He picks up the threads almost happily and is beginning already to adorn the memory of Switzerland with a quiet glamour it never had, and makes more phone calls.

"Yes, marvellous, helped enormously... No, I didn't find a moment to see anyone... No, not lonely... Yes, wonderful... No, not a scrap of work..." The pain is in the gaps between his words, and the gaps are carefully closed boxes he opens only at night.

He is as he had been on the first day back at school. Excited, he flicks through the calendar of events scanning it for new fixtures.

"A competition? I'll see. When's the deadline? Anyway we can talk about it at the meeting."

The competition is a word or two amongst a thousand others at the meeting about an Arts Council grant for refurbishment of the Konjertsaal; new practice rooms for which Baroness Dietzschold has already offered generous support; new seats; new chandelier. As he drives home, the competition is all he remembers.

He is nervous about composing again; is not at all sure. But he could do with the money and has been tipped off about the panel of judges who privately want him to win, considering what he has just lost.

He grows to like Frau Klein where before she had vaguely irritated him. He likes it when her grumpy old body comes through the door. He needs her there, too hideously different from Erike for her presence to upset him. Erike had never cleaned so there is no chance, coming round a corner with coffee in hand, to mistake her stance for his wife's.

He sits at the piano, spreads his hands across the keys soundlessly. Nothing. His desperate mind searches for Erike. Faintly at first, music becomes audible. He echoes it on the piano and then quickly catches the notes onto staves. It is coming. In the evening he listens to Bach, the solemnity soothing his sadness back into place. And he considers, sipping red wine, that a couple of hours a day for a fortnight should do it.

Each morning he plays back what he has done, likes it and adds another page to the folder on the top of the piano.

One of the astounding aspects of Angel is his patience. He has spent three months drilling the cavity clean and now he sits back and watches the hole fill with junk. Mori is chewing on old food; old feelings; making music out of all that is finished; exhausting himself with the complexity of balancing light with dark, fast with slow, right hand with left.

Angel does not interfere; just waits. He is used to unsynchronised responses: raises his eyes and a year later someone looks; whispers in childhood and is heard at death. His life is not measured by time.

At the Akademie they ask him how it is going. He nods easily. They are impressed with his composure and speak in his absence of the Direktor's good judgement in freeing him for three months. And in their agreement is a wave of appreciation that they are artists and can claim that freedom. They are snobs but in this case they are right. Money and talent allow space to mourn privately. When Frau Klein's husband had died she punched her grief into Erike's cushions, polished the silver until it shone the brightest in Bonn, but her life remained dull.

The piece is forty pages long. That makes about ten minutes. Perfect. He carries the score under his arm to the car. He has to hand it to the panel before starting. Sitting in the car, he opens the front page and looks at the dancing notes. He had bought a new rollerball to copy the music out and had enjoyed its silky flow across the paper. The notes are velvet and fluent. He is confident.

The panel is seated. A suited woman looks up to signal they are ready. He stands, silent for a second, and remembers Erike. Then his baton comes down with perhaps more force than necessary, and a round, romantic melody sweeps into the hall and surges up into the domed ceiling. Erike is in the undulations of the music. She is in the swiftness of the violin, for she had been mercurial. She is in the strong bass, for her body had been so firm against his willow tree form as they kissed. Her anger is the pounding, the relentlessness of page seven. Her refreshed face in Austria, the lilting tone of page nine. Page ten is his own grief which Bach and Frau Klein had failed to tidy away.

It is a strange piece. The panel are puzzled. Their minds grasping its pace and speed, note down, 'Nice feel, agile, bright...' But just when the notes are spilling into mental corners reserved for their private concerns, in fact at the point the piece is about to win, the rhythm drags. 'Disappointing,' writes the woman, 'strong beginning... takes us to a dim edge... leaves us dangling...'

The man beside her is technical: 'Poor polyphony.'

The last two members of the panel simply think 'no' and his name is struck from their list. The sole woman judge draws four boxes on her page. Listening to the piece has provided her with criteria she had not had time to identify consciously. Mori, as many a first competitor, is the victim of the panel's busy lives though their judgement is nonetheless fair.

The piece finishes. The audience clap moderately. The ordinary folk are moved, in spite of themselves, by the figure standing to bow. But Mori knows the language of an audience's hands and knows he has not won.

The next two contenders are Dutch. They play impeccably but the panel, leaning forward to confer, agree that they are too indistinguishable to be winners. They are of their country, represent its best qualities, but are not bravely innovative. 'Young after all,' thinks the woman, 'they'll have a chance later on.'

The winner is a woman from Bavaria whose piece is a single mood she has barely felt. She belongs to an age where confessional art is an embarrassment. Kerr Schultz, the senior adjudicator, finally forgets his burglar alarm - which he had not switched on before leaving home and which has been ringing in his head through the Dutch pieces - and is carried for five minutes to Arabia.

It is customary for competitions at the Konjertsaal to end with a two minute rendering of the Founder's Prelude, a piece Mori has never learned because it is so bad. To this everyone will stand before going up to the glass-roofed balcony for drinks.

The Konjertsaal Direktor has forgotten. Damn! He sweats under his suit. He has made several mistakes like this lately. The audience stand ready. No one comes to the piano. He pauses then thinks, 'Lord yes, why not? Mori can do it.' He goes to him as if it is a part of the proceedings and whispers.

"But I don't know the damn thing," Mori whispers back.

"Make something up. It doesn't matter. They won't care."

Mori shrugs and walks to the piano. There is a passive lump of matter in his head. He puts his right hand on the piano. His left stays in his lap. A line of notes stream from his fingers. The audience are interested, then embarrassed. It is a child's tune, a lullaby, and it comes from the jade in him Angel found.

The tune spirals upwards, dispelling the invisible but lingering colours of Arabia and Dutch neatness and Erike.

The Direktor, moved by it, forgets his omission of duty and accompanies the music. High in the room it dances, gathering complexity, and he with it - back on the Mediterranean sands of childhood summers: the shrieks of delight softened by low cloud, packing up for home, straggling up the hill to the car, sandy feet, tight skinned faces from the sun. And all this in an astounding few minutes. Still the audience are standing. And still Mori's left hand rests in his lap.

Angels do not, as in myth, rank themselves in celestial formation making perfect music. Their ears are accustomed to silence. Yet Angel is moved by the tune for it comes from the quiet in the man.

Mori gets up and walks back to his seat. He feels the atmosphere of an audience who are moved but unimpressed. He is a mixture of joy and embarrassment, like an athlete in convalescence stumbling with his first steps when he is used to being applauded as a sprinter.

The Direktor remains standing. Angel moves back to his silence. As he withdraws, he lifts from the room an image of sea and gulls and salt breezes. A wafer thin lightness, his mind can only carry images. The concerns of the audience, he discards before they break his flight.

An idea shimmers on the surface of his mind, ripples his glassy calmness. In the quietness he plays with it; rehearses sitting up, standing, walking in a small body on a small curve of seashore - an island maybe - and feels the joy of being human again. Then he closes into thoughtlessness, for a second's dreaming of life in a body is enough. More, and the standing will be an urgent walk, the island will be a city, and he wishes only for what is special and without pain.

Mori leaves before the prize giving. He wants to take off his bow tie and dinner jacket, put on his Swiss cords and walk into the square under the night sky. As the doorman lets him out he smiles - they greet each other often - and he feels the smile filled with a congratulation his fourth place has not earned him.

He hums through the traffic the tune he had played in the Konjertsaal. He had not needed to learn it, for it has been in him always; and will be the theme of what will later be thought of by the toughest of German critics as his greatest work.

So rapt is he in his humming that he taps to the tune on the accelerator. The lights are red and he hits the car in front. A woman gets out and storms to his window, paper in hand to take his address. He hands it back to her as though offering flowers. The woman is disarmed and does not submit a claim.

The next week Mori is in the Direktor's office discussing a rehearsal schedule. He notices that he is not thanked for stepping in at the last minute. Either the man is embarrassed that a key part of the evening's ceremony was overlooked and wants to forget it, or he does not know what to say about Mori's impromptu tune. Mori is surprised. They are close. He had expected some kind of humorous crack at least. Perhaps he is angry. But he seems calm as he rings through to his secretary to bring him the relevant file. It is as if the incident never happened. And curiously when Mori, lying alone in his large bed late one morning, tries to evoke the tune again he cannot. It has gone.

Gone as a woman goes. Upstairs from the ordinariness of family to the small part of the house that is hers: her dressing table. Takes off her clothes, bathes, dresses for dinner: jewellery, silk, cream-softened skin. When she descends she is not who she was - a snatch of beauty amidst the hair-flying, harassed rush of a person with two lives and only one body to live them - she is wholly beautiful.

So the tune, a snatch only until now, has slipped away to don itself in full melody. Returning, it will occupy first the right hand of a pianist, then a hundred nimble, hardened hands of an orchestra.

And Mori will listen to it, aware that the music is as distinct from the rest of him as jade is distinct from rock and that he has changed (in the way Angel himself once changed); has seen that there are two roads and that he will take the second: will renounce the emotional fruit of his talent, and music will flood into him as balm for minds as tired as his had been. His life will stretch and grow and everyone will have heard of him though the pleasure of fame will somehow be on the other road.

But all that is much later. At present he just lies in his wide bed and dozes. For when an angel works, it just brushes the mind and goes. The jade has been found. Time will do the rest.

And Angel will make ready the fingernail seashore, the velvet wood, the house, the island it had glimpsed in the Konjertsaal which, like all its tasks, had held within it a concealed reward (for only God is an absolute altruist).

The globe is restless with the grey tiredness of fighting for causes that no one can quite grasp. But Angel, attuned only to light, will follow the beams of the Eastern sun and shoot, thoughtlessly like a toddler, legs splayed, down a slide, and land laughing amidst the laughing faces of a mother, a father, who catch it and turn it into a child...

MOTHER

All day her balmy hands have soothed the sick.
at dusk the thick-lipped eucalyptus
lets the sun anoint her with
cool oils.

Kadia stands alone in the warm field and stretches upwards so that her scarf falls back onto her broad shoulders. The cloth nudges into her neck caressing it, and the top of her head, protected by tiny black curls, opens and relaxes. The other women wear their brightly coloured scarves tightly; hers falls and moves with her.

The sun above her head is full of nutrients her woman's body needs. The other women curse at it; their leathery faces turned to the sky; their bodies slanted by yanking children. Kadia's arms hang easily by her side except when she has a basket to fill as now. She bends again from her hips, her large hands cupping the cobs so they snap and drop into the wicker basket in single sweeps. Up and down she goes, pulling and dropping, pulling and dropping, her basket filling, her mind emptying.

When she finishes, she rests for a few seconds then picks her way along the rows of dusty green back to the kraal. Children stand by the roadside as though themselves with child; their stomachs hard bowls of hunger.

Kadia feels full. Not that she isn't hungry. But it doesn't hurt her as it does they who are angry, frenetic, their noses running because their bodies haven't the strength to absorb what little fats they eat. She moves through them back to her hut, the basket clawed at by ten or so hands on the way. Some herbs from her private patch dangle over the edge and she gathers them up as she bends to go through the door. Inside, she puts the basket down and sits at the table.

Kadia has no children. Her body had refused her husband's seed which swum up to her potent and filled so many times. Her womb blocked the makings of a boy child, strong and crazy like him, for she could accommodate no more. Time and again, life after life, she had been a mother. Motherhood ran through and through her so that it had been she whom Nomi, Sirus, Pierre had chosen; she who knew how to hold them and bring out their strangeness until they became extreme and challenging and eventually pushed her away. The hurt of that; of being chosen then rejected, had made her womb contract.

It is also a gift, for there is no bitterness in her; no sudden flash of nastiness on her features, such as spoils the most beautiful face; no hidden sorrow that makes her turn away jealously as gaggles of little ones fly to their mothers. Her mind and body move easily as one who has completed a task and is blessed.

The clay walls of her hut make a soft peaceful darkness which matches her unburdened body. She has made her home like herself and is happy to rest in it indefinitely, for there is no call on her now that she has passed sixty. There are days when she just sits and sits and follows the spider's journey up to the rounded ceiling, second by second. She wonders sometimes why it turns off its track; what impulse in its tiny body deflects it. A lump in the clay maybe, like the ridges in a leaf which give rain its road.

She especially loves the hut in the wet season. She loves the smell and the hush. The whole kraal changes: the children's games change, the food changes, the sleeping times change; everything. In these months the atmosphere is heated and restless and the women easily flare up, exhausted in their efforts to keep body and soul together. Still, it is quiet; and the quietness is of days, months, years...

Unless it is broken as today by a police noise.

The police come in the daytime now, the pleasure of scaring the natives out of sleep having worn thin. Anyway they are too lazy to wait up. Daytime will do. They are trying to clean the place up, whatever that means.

It is a little pocket of violence. Most of it has subsided, but for a whim and the old bug flares up in a place unnoticed by the media. Squeezed into one corner it is nastier; like a body cured of disease except for one pinch of poison, compact and lethal.

The Inspector, responding to the poison as a jagged line of acidity in his stomach, thinks, 'We'll clean up that place,' as though it is his cupboard which overflows with the yellow pages of outdated books.

The woman in the hut next to Kadia's freezes. Her guts stretch and tighten. Her children are outside. Kadia doesn't move either, but she is serene, her stomach a warm balanced sack in her centre. They will not touch her. They will walk into her dark, silent hut, look, walk out as if the room were empty and she, large and solid on her kitchen chair, were not there in front of them; not even take the food; not even lift the pots off the table and then slam them down swearing. Deflected, they will not even speak. It happens so many times that she knows she is safe as a fisherman knows that the sea will never go beyond its highest tide line. They do rape old women, but it will not happen to her.

She can hear screams outside; wants to rush out and help, yet knows she can never interfere. Even when the old men try to intercede they never survive.

She has so many times seen the struggling skinny torso of a child held upside down between two men as a third pushes the mother back inside her hut, guts it for food, checks her ration book, pushes her into the darkness and abuses her; has as many times measured the shock that follows each raid; has watched how for days afterwards the children's games are jumpy and bad-tempered and how the women withdraw into their huts, needing solitude as again for the tenth, eleventh time they try to rebuild the inside of their homes and bodies.

She moves to the doorway to look out, but before her face is under the sun, she hears, "Okay boys," and a disbanding, a departure. The children, released like springs, leap to their dry-breasted mothers who are still beautiful but for broken teeth which show now in relieved smiles interspersed with loud cursing.

Kadia sits down again. She has no part to play in their recovery. The women have each other. Scooping a child up, holding it, taking it to its mother, is no longer in her; though innate compassion moved her to the door. It is as if she lives somewhere else and everyone knows as day follows night there will only be silence around her. She is older after all and that too is on the side of her solitude. The younger ones live in dense proximity. Their jangled nerves wrap around each other in an angry and protective cluster so that their men returning from the mines find it difficult to reach them.

Sometimes they speak about her but not much. And when what they say fuses and rushes in an upsurge of malice, the wind sweeps their words over the dry veld that borders the kraal.

"What's that noise?" Kadia turns from her stillness. A child comes through her door, slapping its feet on the cool mud and sits down as though in its own hut. After all each hut is much the same; but not, for each woman has her smell, each place its atmosphere.

Large-kneed, thin-ankled, the boy dangles his legs from the chair and looks at her. 'Wants food, or recovery from the raid,' Kadia supposes. But no, he is not eyeing her shelves, does not seem about to ask; just wants some peace; a rest from the hullabaloo outside.

He gets up and lies on the grass mat, rolling and humming; stops, pulls out an interfering peanut from his pants, puts it on the table, and goes out. Then returns to the doorway, small and smiling, and runs off again. Kadia takes the nut and shells it. She strolls towards the door and sits down leaning against its smoothened surface. The child has drawn her out; made her aware of the fragile thread that ties her to these people.

She is not lonely. She is not seeking any comfort in this move; is like a tree merely, leaning to the wind. The child blew in and now she leans; moves outwards to the villagers and into the sun that warmed her earlier.

The days are so long, so hot and unbroken. The sun seems to soften as some women cluster indifferently around a toddler in the dust trying to get something out of his foot. Eventually they get it and the released child falls backwards. It hurts but at least the hurt is different from the hurt in his stomach; less of an ache and quick to remove. He limps back to the other children and their eyes take her in innocently as they span the dusty yard that is their communal garden.

She begins to doze as they cannot, for tension keeps their brains tight and alert. Her head drops onto her wide chest. She is dreaming; nothing shaped or vivid but a sensation of running, carrying water in a weightless pot on her head and running, running, grass tickling her legs. The young women dream of old age, of struggling away from hands grabbing at their straight torsos, and she dreams of loping towards someone somewhere who is waiting to shower her with flowers. She has done nothing; has lived, eaten, slept, moved to old age in this one place; but in perpetual separation from its harshness.

Many times, in other births, women have clustered around this mother and said, 'You shouldn't take it! Why do you put up with it? He's a scoundrel. Painting, mon Dieu...! Preaching, my God...! He doesn't care about you, does he?' Or of Lily: 'She's disgracing you!' Each time she, who had served as a mother more than any other relationship, had renounced her friendships believing them to be less important than the strange extremism of her child.

Now because of her sacrifice, she is getting a rest: a private harmony; the greater for being amidst horror and for going unnoticed by those around her who are unhappy and can only see themselves. Her days are a gentle swing backwards and forwards rather than a series of brave leaps. And she deserves it, for she has spent many lives leaping.

It is a reward so marked that she knows that the police will not touch her; that if the riots start again she will be guided through them. And she assimilates all of that simply in a single wave of comfort over her sleeping skin as though her head is held in the soft hollow of a shoulder.

And the reward is not from God, nor from the children who have tugged her soul and body through motherhood, for they cannot protect her now, being busy in their own completion. It is life itself which is rewarding her, for it too has its logic though the consciousness of single births at a time make it nearly impossible to see.

The children are drawn instinctively out of their dry mischief into her orbit. Their games veer towards her so that stones thrown make dust fly around her and their laughter circles her.

Kadia wakes from her doze refreshed by the water she carried in her sleep. It has cleansed her of the sensations of stretch and bend, loving, ageing, walking. She wipes her hand across her soft black lids, her cheeks, large-lobed ears; then looking inside to her heart, her lungs, her stomach, she restores each to harmony. She wants to rest in the gentle pose sleep has brought, but one of the women is coming over to her. She is whimpering.

"What is it, Amman?" Kadia asks.

"Not got nothin' now," blubbers the woman. "Not him, her, nothin'."

"What you mean?" Kadia again.

Kadia's voice is a touch hard, protecting herself from the woman's intrusion - as her child of other births had always protected itself from hers. Right now she does not want any gripes. Selfish, maybe, but this is her heaven and no one should break its simplicity.

But inside her is the lightness of the rewarded, and Amman has come for that, for her life is a punishment. She has heard from her neighbour's eldest son that her husband has been taken by the police for rape and her children are fighting, her boy jerking his pelvis backwards and forwards in a terrifying miniature dumb show. He is six.

"Day in, day out, they're scrappin'," whines Amman. She looks to them for some support and, apart from the six year old, "they're old enough aren't they?" He, the bastard man, has been nothing but trouble. He only ever wanted her body not her soul and "my soul cryin' now Kadia, my soul cryin'."

Kadia remains firm. It is an old story; it is everyone's story. But today it has blown up in Amman's heart and made her shake her boy and cry, 'Not my fault your daddy don't bring no food, not my fault. Stop hollerin' like a madman, stop it!' And she has walked straight out to Kadia on the step with the cool dark of the hut behind her.

Kadia gets up and goes inside knowing the woman will follow. Amman is thin; the breasts under her shirt hang long. She is forty or so though she looks both very much older, fifty, sixty, and very much younger, twelve, thirteen. She speaks like the latter.

Kadia looks at her body and remembers hearing the woman's screams ringing across the kraal as she gave birth to one, two, three, four. She has been becoming more closed lately not giving her body so easily to her husband any more, because it hurt:

"Kadia, it hurts me so much, I think I goin' to die." So he has been leaving her for longer periods and now has got himself into trouble. "Bastard man!" Kadia knows her story.

Amman does not look like a mother; does not have the roundness that is the result of something big and sacrificing that swells the body, makes each limb a receptacle for a child's need: shoulder for a pillow, neck for the full-throated shout of reprimand, back big and wide for carrying a curled sleeping body.

'She's a child herself,' thinks Kadia, not cross now. She makes her sit at the table, then on the floor. She knows what is needed. She knows the woman needs a whack on her back, a loud word and then a big hug. She knows that it is time to let down her reserve. This woman is desperate; her sorrow so heavy that her mind is buckling and, like the children, has come to Kadia with her heart a begging bowl. And Kadia fills it.

She does what she has always done; when Nomi taunted her, when Sirus walked out on her, when Pierre pushed away his drink... she becomes stable, giving what is needed. Yet underneath, she lets herself be exploited by their needs. And Amman is as cunning and angular as the rest of them and Kadia slips into the old pattern unawares.

"Well, looks like you gotta help them children get used to not having a papa. Looks like that's what you gotta do. Then you gotta give 'em a good shake and tell 'em they got to help you and then... you gotta get yourself another man because man means food."

The woman looks at her, shock making her cheekbones stick out and her eyes shut to the idea.

"I can't," she says. "I can't give my body 'gen."

"You'll just have to."

The conversation becomes a tight twist of rope between them. Kadia, observing Amman's desperation, lets go, gives in. And in that relaxation of effort, all the light that is in her comes out from her eyes and goes to Amman. Her spirit, nurtured and silent for all those years, empties itself into the woman.

"Yep, that's what you gotta do," repeats Kadia, her words now holding no force. Amman stops moaning and sits up.

"Maybe you're right, but not yet, not yet. Not for a year, two years. My heart bangin' with anger Kadia, bangin', bangin'." She is energetically beating her chest. "Am gonna wait a while, then see. What you got in there?" She is looking at the pots on the fire. Kadia fetches them and scoops mealymeal and stew into a bowl. Amman slurps quick fingerfuls in the darkness, while Kadia looks at her bent head. She had been looking forward to her lunch. Irritation rises in her as she fetches a second bowl, but she regrets it seeing the speed and noise of the woman filling her stomach and puts it back, her hands moving without her mind agreeing.

The stew enters Amman like a draught of medicine; slides down into her stomach like nothing she makes in her hut, for she cannot be bothered cutting and peeling.

"Good, good," she sighs, her eyes clearer. She looks at Kadia closely for the first time and leaves.

She comes back the next day and the next and the next. And with each visit Kadia slips further and further into the mothering groove.

"No, no, not like that," she says to Amman who has come with a new idea about her son whose obscene gestures are getting worse.

"No, you not gonna stop him like that. You gotta give him somethin' new to play with." She laughs at her own obscenity. And when Amman questioningly tilts her head, Kadia goes to the back of the hut and brings out a thick stick of wood.

"This'll do it. Give him this."

"What's that then?"

"It's not nothin'. But you got to pretend it somethin' and he'll take it. You gotta give it him like it is the witchman's wand, then he'll forget himself and play with that. You try."

"What about her? She as bad! Hollerin' all night, from moment her head go down to mornin'."

"Well, you kissed her? Kissed her before she go down?"

"Hates her. She a big pain in my chest, all her screamin'."

"Kiss her, kiss her, that's what."

Advice comes out of her as easy as water pouring and Amman drinks and drinks though it leaves Kadia empty and a little tired.

A month later, Kadia is in the fields. It is nearly midday and she wants a sit down. She puts her basket beside her and lies back on the side of the road.

She is almost asleep when she hears the sound of women laughing in the distance. The laughter becomes louder. She sits up. Six or so are walking towards her though they have not seen her. Amman is one of them. She has her arm in the air and Kadia can see that she is holding the stick she has given her. The laughter reaches a climax as Amman dances the wood in the air. Kadia hears her name. It comes to her in a singsong of abuse and then more laughter.

She feels the energy drain out of her but at the same time sharp and alert as if something has hit her. It is a sign. Her old soul recognises something hidden in this little group in the sunlight: she has given too much and must be careful. Leaning on one arm she watches them pass by. Their walk is fast and strong and punctuated with an occasional leap as first one then another plays at grabbing the wooden baton. They are like their own children whom they scold and hit, their energy as high and teetering. And in a split second she realises it is her energy.

But when a day later Amman comes crying, saying that she cannot bear it much longer, that her child was saying such things in his sleep like somethin' has got into him, Kadia resumes her warmth, slapping the woman's back and feeding her, moved again by her desperation.

The Inspector's stomach begins to hurt badly. A ruthlessness strikes him: 'Clear that place completely. Clear it forever.' Midday, the men swerve into the village. Kadia is usually in her hut at this time, back from the fields sitting quietly, but she is walking slowly in the hot sun, her basket a little heavy though it holds the same few cobs of green and sprig of herbs as always.

As she approaches the kraal she senses panic. Something is up. She recognises the quiet between screams as they concentrate on somebody. In a minute they will be out of the hut, shouting again, before converging on the next. The pattern is so frighteningly repetitive. Except she is here not in her hut; she is exposed in the bright heat. They will be out in a second. No time to get to her hut first unless she runs and that will attract attention. Still, what else is there? It is so hot. She puts her basket down in the yard gently, slowly, with some of her old calm. It touches the dust and she moves like a man through fire, confident that he will not get burnt because he has made his livelihood from this feat. That is how it has always been... But suddenly they are out, a spearhead of energy leaping towards her.

She stands alone, tiny under the sun. Then in a spurt of terror she leaps into the air and runs; a few steps only and they are with her, on her.

It takes not a minute. She is old after all. One fist in her stomach and she is down, away. The men look at each other asking with nods and gestures whether to bother any further with her. The sun surges, and they decide not to. They clear out leaving the body flat on the ground.

Through the grey peace that is the waiting time before life resumes; when the soul resolves itself in the silence: rebalancing, reshaping, visiting if necessary to say sorry, or to hurt, Kadia's spirit moves. It is a peaceful glide upwards away from the dust and heat, for her life has been a good one and there is little to settle.

A beam twists and tips Kadia into peace. She sees again the moment of her death. Hears again the noise of the police: what's that? What is it? Her mind panics, the more vivid in its reactions for being free of a body.

"God, they'll kill me! Help, my God! Amman! Bastards!" And mentally she recreates her own struggling torso; receives again the pummel of fists on the breasts she no longer has.

But it is not bastards, it is God. He makes the cobs and herbs scatter in slow motion on the stone; has her arms and legs tip and tumble like soft wool supported by hands as her form is lowered. He softens and changes her death so that the shock will not blemish her future. For he loves her, loves her unequivocally. In some ways even more than Christ. Christ gave himself once whilst she, unknown, unremembered, has given herself time and again.

    He lifts her high inside an arc of light, like a star held in a curve of moon. And she rests.

CHILD

Unnoticing, the children played in the garden
as tremoring roots
took hold of the house.

But Angel, attuned only to light, will follow the beams of the Indian Ocean sun and will shoot thoughtlessly like a toddler, legs splayed, down a slide...

She has come so far. She has lived so long. Her face has been the face of a man, a woman, a child - unwieldy, awkward, delicate, angular, soft. And now she is a girl on an island, smoothed like stone by sea into seeming simplicity. Having known so much, she now knows nothing, but that it is morning and the sun is rising. While above her is not only the sun but a tiny sparkle of light: which is Fire-Fly.

She wakes excited without knowing why. Something is different; the different of womanhood descending gently in the night, her breasts budding, her hips forming. Yet, too, it is her mind which is shifting and slipping like the sand into a dip, ready not to conceive but to receive. The two, after so many lives of loving, are easy to confuse.

She rolls over and enjoys the stretch of her limbs into a new shape. The sun dances petals on her bedroom ceiling and the skylight is turquoise blue with the promise of a fine day. Her feeling is a part of that fineness, for here on this island where she seemed brought not born, she is in tune with the elements. Nature is kind; the sea laps its protection against all that is mainstream, mainline.

In the next door house, her cousin lies. He is the same age and make as her, his skin the same gold, his hair the same black, his soul marked with similar scars. He is Jamil and she Amba, named, as their cries sung like two staves of music on the air by parents who hoped they would live in tune.

From childhood they have played together and in the innocent choosing of similar stones, leaves, trees to climb, the footholds of their spirits have been shared. Today he too wakes, feeling the tide of his love for Amba rise to a fullness. Today it will overflow into words, touch. Her face comes before him as if she were there. He tries out her features with his own. His eyes slip into hers, his mouth echoes her morning smile and his body lies in the same curve, as he faces the window listening to the sea's soft breath against the shore.

Less than a thousand miles away, a man in London is slumped in an armchair, a piece of paper on his corduroy lap and without knowing why he writes down a list of sins. There is not much to write. He has slapped his son twice and married the same number of times. Other things were just part of being human; the shared sins of everyone. Yet hurting your own child, not just in one physical movement but in the constant subtle undermining of its confidence, that was probably the worst thing he had done, and seeing it in blue-biroed writing slanting backwards, he feels depressed.

He lies down and dozes, dreaming that he stabs a boy. When he wakes, his first thought is how easy it was and that what had been a mere slap to his child might once have been an act of real violence; that behind this small remembered sin was a great deal much worse: acts of an unknown past, weighing like a dark heaviness. He slices potatoes and cuts a finger. The phone rings and he stumbles when he should be cool and informed.

This glimpse of the past has come as a nudge, a gift. The man is not quite sure if he wants to accept the gift, which he suspects his empty head has picked up neurotically. Should an angel come to land in his kitchen, and say, "Mr Taylor, I have the accounts here (holding out a silver embossed manual) of everything you have ever done. If you would care to give it a glance, your future will be blessed," he might have accepted it gracefully, rather than by default. He does not realise that this is how gifts often come, riding on the back of currents already in motion.

It is mid-morning. They sit in the sun making patterns in the white sand. He draws a circle, she a vertical through it, he a horizontal, she a diagonal, he another. It is a wheel.

Their fingers move with the deftness of artists making pictures for posterity. Here on this sunspot they have sketched animals, people, houses, pathways, but in recent months their pictures have been shapes - the organs of their own bodies or of earth's misshapen lands - portrayed in the grains.

The circle pleases them. They sit waiting for the rising water to flow in and out of the lines and take it. It is coming, coming, the first drop touching the circumference and then softly flooding into the circle. Jamil turns his face to hers. There is a warmth in his cheeks as though a secret has burst onto his mind and she has lifted it out of his eyes.

Now they are walking. They want to hold hands but do not because Jamil enjoys more the vibrant space of a gesture withheld and Amba fears the space - that precious part of her so often possessed - being filled too soon. So they move from the shore to the woods, seeking in the vocabulary of their spirits a love gesture which is new.

Under a canopy of green they watch stripes of shadow ripple up the trees. They want to talk but there is nothing to say because the treasure of their spirits has bypassed their minds and moved straight into their arms, their legs, their wide faces.

Impulses ripple like water through their bodies and come to rest behind the velvet lids of their eyes. He touches a tree as if it is her. She traces its bark rings with her fingers as if here in this layered oldness an answer will come as to why her heart feels such anticipation. Something more important than love will happen today.

The man, who feels insight as a knot in his head, lies back down again. There is nothing else to do. Normally there are a hundred things onto which he can project his mood. But now they are not there, or else his body is too weak to go to them. He knows there is nothing but stillness, silence and confrontation that can help him, and the easiest way to get stillness is to sleep. He curls into a ball on his side and feels the ruts in the counterpane press into his cheek.

Their families run by the gentle rhythm that nature runs by: the fall of the leaves, the eclipse of the moon. They know without speaking when to party and when to be quiet, when to wake and when sleep. They have no clocks.

The meal is a splash of colour and form: whites, reds, greens; fruits, flowers, leaves. Their island is a fertile little planet of its own, suspended above earth or at its unseen heart. They know of the events of the world out to sea, but their consciousness seems sealed against its sorrow.

Their two fathers stand at the window. They have about them the dignity of generals who have remembered the precision not the wounds of battle. They are simple but their eyes are ancient, know nuances of feeling as clearly as they know the colours, shapes and forms of the buildings that structure their island village.

Joining them to eat, Amba and Jamil seek refuge in the peace of the carefully laid table, their gaze sliding away from each other as if in the meeting of their eyes there is dynamite.

Out to sea a ship passes. They watch it and so each other, meeting in the tiny criss-cross of rigging and the lines of its grey decks. It could be a battleship but from here it is only a toy, a thankful diversion from a feeling they can barely contain because it is bigger than love.

After the meal, the men play a game. Their long, wise fingers slide wooden pieces across a board with the seriousness and silence of politicians plotting a redistribution of resources. Today Amba finds the game cold. Her father is beautiful, she can watch for hours the crisp folds of his shirt, the perfect arc of his back as he bends to straighten the patterned cloth around his waist. But today he is a straight line along which she wishes to entwine flowers.

"Come on, man, come on! Move!" But he cannot. His whole body is anchored, heavy, pressing him there, as the body sometimes will to give the mind time for realisation. But he realises nothing except that he is sorry he has hit his child. It had not been easy without a wife, and with an overpowering sense of being only half-successful, half-attractive, half-clever, and seeing the same mediocrity in his child stumbling over his reading, he had hit: "Come on, Ben! Come on! You can do better than that, can't you..." The boy had not cried, but now the man does. He cries into the counterpane.

He wonders what he can do. He tries desperately to think of a person whom he can talk to; with whom he can sit in a room, surrounded by possessions that are not his, and his back bent forwards to confide his muddle and it not matter. But whoever he thinks of might understand some of it but not all of it; the guilt but not the emptiness, the emptiness but not the fear, the regret but "for Christ's sake, not listing your sins on a spiral notepad!" If he were to choose a woman, she might think he were choosing her, and if a man, he might be flippant. His mind is like a cheap toy expelling light plastic balls that rattle and roll uselessly onto the ground. His thoughts multiply and miss their target, and he feels stale and wasted.

Jamil is swimming. He too prefers the fluidity of movement to the manoeuvring of chessmen. He is swimming away the surge of energy he feels, though the water invigorates him so that, running into the shallows he is a Greek statue animated, vivacious and graceful.
Amba, moving for a moment by the rhythm not of time but desire, sees him and cannot help herself. She goes to him and her light, searching touch on his skin wet with the sea is as the passing of a hand across an electric fence. The sun gleams white hot and the sand glares up at them. Her body - carrying along its nerves the messages of a thousand years - suddenly alerts her to a danger. She leaps away her feet slipping on the sand so that it takes a long time to make any headway. Jamil looks after her, his gaze stretching out to caress, but his body is a statue again, unable even to smile.
Slants of gold play on the water and amidst them sparkles. Above, Fire-Fly echoes the shine and tosses and turns in an ecstasy of freedom.

He walks up Shaftesbury Avenue - lonely. The shops are shut. His body feels exceedingly old as he walks, and his trousers, recently bought seem gloomy and heavy. Even if he had stood in the warm frothing fragrance of a jacuzzi he would have looked through the water and seen his skin white, his hips uneven. He is that low. But a last reserve of strength impels his legs; and their movement, steady and slow, give his mind a rhythm to think by.
He feels as though there is nothing left to discover; that at every corner (he has turned into Piccadilly) there will be a face, a building, a movement of the wind that he has seen or felt before. He challenges himself to find a flicker of hope amidst the dullness, a temporary lift, a "that'd be nice, yes that would change things..."
A noise. He turns. A gang of youths from nowhere. There is a

random nastiness about them. They are bored, aimless, made of the grey of the pavement they spend their time scuffling. He feels repulsed not afraid. Their swearing is devoid of real obscenity; is an indistinct murkiness out of which only physical violence can lift them. And when it happens - in a crotch kneed - it is so unsurprising that everyone walks on, though the fourteen year-old victim reels in agony, purple spots dancing in front of his eyes.

The man walks on too, but the scene has disturbed him. He makes the connections of a paranoid: he is responsible, it is his violence being enacted by these boys.

And touching this possibility is like skimming his fingers across an electric fence. It has always been there, buzzing away in the background. And it frightens him, for everyone in his life - except his wife who had leant over his face at night and seen it register the anger of unfulfilled desire - had said what a good man he was. But he is not a particularly good man.

She runs and runs like an animal in flight, to a rock on the other side of the island and lies trembling on the warm stone. It feels to her only like the catching of breath after an exertion, but it is a deeper fear she is dealing with; the fear of having led Jamil - gentle, thought-free, without will - into the sacred recess of her mind, which, a second away from completion, is vulnerable. She ranges around herself, touching, feeling, and the calming of her silken stomach, golden and flat in the sun tells her that all is well, she has avoided the deliciousnes of a snare that later could become hatred or loss.

Exhausted, she sleeps. And Fire-Fly twists and turns in the sunbeams that lightly finger her face. Soon. She is already calm and old enough - so old - to allow it its freedom. She only need trust that time has its hand in this. Then she will be light. And Fire-Fly will return to her.

When she wakes up, Amba feels a hundred years have passed, leaving only seconds in which to prepare herself. At home, her mother lays out crimson silk on her bed, though to her knowledge there is no party tonight.

The man has only walked a hundred yards on, when he sees police amongst the young men.

'Good, they're dealing with it.'

He feels as a child does when the whole class is to blame for an incident. It is everyone's fault. His mood is part of a whole swing downwards of which his spiral notepad is just a symptom.

The police tell the lads to go home. Their uniformed bodies contain the struggle of colour and movement, and the man does the same with his mood. Tells himself to get on home. 'It's Sunday, that's made you morbid.' Sunday, the butt of a thousand curses.

On return, he finds he has locked himself out. He has to knock on the caretaker's door. Waiting on the landing in the dark - it is March, grey, the place smells of old sofas - his mind has painful access to a panorama of all his nicest memories: dinner, warmth, brown skin, the feel of sand, sea, sneaking out to meet her in Harrods. The thoughts are miserably unsynchronised with the shabbiness around him.

The caretaker gives the key to the man as though he is a nuisance; a child who should be more organised. And because the man is feeling vulnerable he says sorry too many times. When he is finally inside, he has an urge to clean out the flat from top to bottom, but lacking the energy, instead opens the fridge.

He takes out some cheese. Its solid yellowness comforts him. Cut by a wire into a neat wedge, it makes precision look easy. He starts to think, as he eats in jagged bites, of the next day. Not of the appointments or contracts, the letters or phone calls, but of the coffee on his desk, steaming hot, placed carefully. It makes him feel mothered.

When he goes to sleep, he meets fear repeatedly and wakes himself up three times. Then just lies, curled and a bit cold, listening to the shrill dawn chorus.

The houses are filled with light. Formality has lifted like dust and the two families brightly mingle over small things. They have dressed up, the men in stiff shirts, the women in rainbow silks. Wafts of rose and musk and music come from the verandah where the chimes play in the wind. They have, in this tiny secluded place, forgotten culture. Birdsong, the swish of the sea, the night stars are their pictures and music. They have worked hard for this: days, years, spent with cheeks rested against chapel walls perfecting the hollow of Christ's cheek, the soft curve of Mary's blue robe. They have played the note A a thousand times to hear its different resonances. Creativity is in their bones.

The evening is a silken ribbon thrown into an endless ripple and Fire-Fly, liking the shine, slips up and down, its pure energy making everyone at dinner sparkle with laughter and mischief. Jamil's father loosens his shirt and his smile seems to stretch the length and breadth of the room.

A force has been gathering in Amba's mind. In the morning a tiny billow, it is now a wave. It is to do with Jamil and yet it is not, for when she turns to her mother the feeling is still there. It is everywhere like an event touching a whole land.

She pushes back her chair. Her face is hot. Behind her laughter she is concerned. Something will go wrong; something will spoil the beautiful intimacy of this evening. Their innocent impertinences, the bold openness of their speech will slip into indiscretion. She senses their teetering on the edge of error. But that teetering is only the passing of a shadow, the light falling of a feather compared to the dark-winged eagle that hovers over the man in London.

Jamil feeling her unease looks at her. 'We can play like this,' his eyes say, while hers say, 'We cannot, we cannot.' She wants to leave, to get up and walk in the fresh air. To be alone. But she has always done that. Always. Always she has got up and left. For intimacy and formality have never rested easily within her. Instead, she sits and watches Jamil as he leans back in his chair. A shiver of chauvinism crosses his face and then leaves like the last of something that was once his strength.

He suddenly appears so trusting, not dynamite but flowers in his eyes. And looking at that bare, open face, her fear calms after his, like waves flattening one after the other. They have reached gold, are positioned together in a patch of light.

And upon that gold - its safest runway - Fire-Fly lowers itself gently, slowly, delicately and slips into the silent, sculpted space in Amba's mind which has been the home of so many. Fire-Fly, the abhorrer of mediocrity, dependence, compromise; and yet, in whose absence made the soul of Nomi, Sirus, Corina... victim to just that, so that everyone met became for a while this missing piece. Fire-Fly, sparkling for so long above, is back in its old, gold setting.

And Amba feels the bliss of completion.

The next day the man goes to sit in Westminster Cathedral; an act of reverence he has not observed since his student days. Being his own boss, he is free to come and go from the office. Sometimes he wishes he were just an employee. Responsibility is lonely. It would be nice sometimes to be told to pay the bills, and then be thanked and rewarded with, "Good job, good man. Well done!" But no one will say that to him. He has to tell others. And when he forgets, they grow careless and critical and go home at five twenty-five.

He sits down near the middle of the cathedral. He notices there are lots of people there. Are they tourists or have they come to pray? The atmosphere tells him that they have not just come to look at the font, the altar, the floors paved with tombs of saints. They are troubled in the way he is.

He shuffles and then wonders what to do. The man does not disbelieve in God, but he finds the prayer embarrassing. He wants to talk about sin and loneliness but does not know how to put it, or what to do. He looks at the woman to his right. She is sitting, eyes closed, seemingly in conversation. Little smiles come and go, as though punctuating her prayer: 'Yes, God, yes, I know. Yes, I have done that. That's complete...' An eyebrow lifts as though God is telling her a nasty little secret about someone. 'Really?' her eyebrow says. 'Well, we knew that didn't we...' And it sickens him: it is glib and complacent. And she probably wouldn't cook dinner for her sick mother.

It is night. Amba and Jamil stand on the verandah alone and facing each other like two trees that have grown side by side, their roots entwined, over a long, long time. Fire-Fly now resting within her, Amba has the confidence of eternity in her eyes, and is happy to stand forever.

She takes from her pocket a love token; a gold coin she had found in the sand. Slipping on her dress before dinner she had seen it amongst the decorations for her hair. She had put it in her pocket feeling in its weight a safety.

She presses it now into Jamil's palm. Her fingers are strong like a mind making a point, though the coin is cool and smooth and simple.

He looks down and sees it like a tiny planet imprinted on his palm. Where heart lines, head lines, life lines were, there is now a circle. He feels an immense pleasure rise through his body. In the pressing of her fingers and the shine of the gold is a hushed acceptance.

Glancing back through the window, Amba sees the faces of mother and father and mother and father smiling and watching and sharing this intimacy. Their eyes are encouraging. And instantly these figures, with their dignity and carefulness, are with them on the verandah. And they dance. All of them. Their bodies moving in graceful formation under the full moon.

The silence of the cathedral which seems to have shut him out, is softened by the flicker of candles as he passes the little side chapel on his way out. He hesitates and lets his mind be soothed by a light that is natural and fragile; different from the distilled clarity of prayer. Suddenly he feels grateful as if he has touched upon what made him come here. The cathedral is too big, the chapel holds sacred the bones of saints too good for him, but the candles give him hope.

A softness enters his eyes and walking back to his office he feels light and clear as he requests his secretary to deflect any calls.

He picks up a spiral notepad from his in-tray. He fills one page and then another. He is writing fast and thoughtlessly in an easy continuation of what now lies crumpled and covered with egg shell in his kitchen bin: a shopping list of sins. He scans each page as he writes, and as the book fills, he feels a lightness - akin, he pauses to reflect, to the feeling that follows a confession in church. But it is different, for the man leaving the confession box feels his sins swathed around him - tight clothes loosened simply - while the man in the office feels laughter welling up. 'I'm a bad man,' he explodes, like a child. And he reads back his sins with the interest of a person reading a good novel. And again he is filled by an overwhelming urge to laugh but he remembers the secretary behind the opaque door and checks himself. Not for long. The laughter breaks through his reserve, as the island magic has broken through time and space to reach him. The laughter of relief; he is being freed. He had reached rock bottom, but here in his office he is being freakishly forgiven. And forgiveness does not mean accepting a penalty, but a total obliteration of the past. He feels like an animal lifted out of a rusty trap it has dragged around for half its life.

Jamil comes to her room as naturally as the moonlight shines across the landing.
They move as water rushing over stones, as flowers bursting open in warmth. They need nothing from each other and so they receive everything: the touch, the slow - eternally slow - rise of desire, the gentle shudder as waves break over them again and again; the release, the gentleness, the abandoned relax.
And afterwards lying in the coolness, blissfully separate again, Amba slips like a clear stream back into thought. 'I am not alone then,' she thinks, her past painting itself briefly upon this space of night silence. And Jamil's breath seems to her now, as he lies asleep beside her, like the quiet voice of the eternal but invisible presence of Fire-Fly.

On his way home from the office, the man buys flowers for his son who has returned from a week-end with his mother, has let himself in after school and is trying to find a missing piece from his model under his bed. He had it on Friday and now it is gone. He hears his father approach the door and fiddle with the lock, and has the wildest thought that maybe daddy has brought him a present, and maybe it is a model. Instead, there is the fragrance of roses in his face and his father hugging him.
The boy is too young for flowers but he registers the change in the busy man's behaviour; tastes it in the mashed potatoes at supper which for the first time since mummy and daddy split up are not lumpy. And after supper they go for a walk by the river. The lights on the water jump and flicker and the man wants to take his son's hand, but thinks maybe he is too old for that, so he puts his arm around his bony shoulders man to man, and they look into the floating restaurants and at Big Ben gleaming over the water. It is so good.

The sun touches Amba's eyelids before it reaches Jamil's. She looks at his arm stretched across the bed, the soft skin of his wrists and the curl of his artist's fingers. She traces his shoulder, the base of his neck, his ear. Where others have only shameless plains of muscle and bone, he has, in the lines of his body, tiny dips in which to hide secrets. And so has she. The space under her arm is a cave, the triangle at her neck a dark cavern, for she too has had things to hide. And now Fire-Fly has lightened and smoothed her.

She lies back down, the sun full on her face. Instinct whispers that nothing can harm her now; that even if the house were to fall down, the island to merge, the continent to splinter; even if there were screaming and shouting around her, she would remain. She will be safe as she has not been for so much of her existence, for dependence has always endangered her. But the only thought in a mind which is not aware of the real light it carries is, 'This warm sun. I love it!'